SPECIAL MESSAGE TO READERS

This book is published under the auspices of
THE ULVERSCROFT FOUNDATION
(registered charity No. 264873 UK)

Established in 1972 to provide funds for research, diagnosis and treatment of eye diseases. Examples of contributions made are: —

A new Children's Assessment Unit at Moorfield's Hospital, London.

•

Twin operating theatres at the Western Ophthalmic Hospital, London.

•

A Chair of Ophthalmology at the University of Leicester.

•

The establishment of a Royal Australian College of Ophthalmologists "Fellowship".

You can help further the work of the Foundation by making a donation or leaving a legacy. Every contribution, no matter how small, is received with gratitude. Please write for details to:

**THE ULVERSCROFT FOUNDATION,
The Green, Bradgate Road, Anstey,
Leicester LE7 7FU, England.
Telephone: (0116) 236 4325**

**In Australia write to:
THE ULVERSCROFT FOUNDATION,
c/o The Royal Australian College of
Ophthalmologists,
27, Commonwealth Street, Sydney,
N.S.W. 2010.**

BORDER KILL

He stepped down from the train to a town in the grip of something far more than a bleak mid-winter. The folk of Remark were waiting in dread of news of the notorious Doone gang crossing the border after their latest bank raid and taking refuge amongst them. But there was one man who was expecting the stranger, who knew the dark secret of his past, and the reason why he was here — simply willing the Doones to hit town.

*Books by Dan Claymaker
in the Linford Western Library:*

HENNIGAN'S REACH
HENNIGAN'S LAW

DAN CLAYMAKER

BORDER KILL

Complete and Unabridged

LINFORD
Leicester

First published in Great Britain in 1996 by
Robert Hale Limited, London

First Linford Edition
published 1998
by arrangement with
Robert Hale Limited, London

The right of Dan Claymaker to be identified
as the author of this work has been asserted
by him in accordance with the
Copyright, Designs and Patents Act, 1988

Copyright © 1996 by Dan Claymaker
All rights reserved

British Library CIP Data

Claymaker, Dan
 Border kill.—Large print ed.—
Linford western library
 1. Western stories
 2. Large type books
 I. Title
 823.9'14 [F]

ISBN 0–7089–5190–2

Published by
F. A. Thorpe (Publishing) Ltd.
Anstey, Leicestershire

Set by Words & Graphics Ltd.
Anstey, Leicestershire
Printed and bound in Great Britain by
T. J. International Ltd., Padstow, Cornwall

This book is printed on acid-free paper

For D.W.M.
a newsman in the
grand tradition

1

THE REMARK BUGLE
Territory of North Dakota

Friday, January 7th, 18–

BANK RAID AT LASSERTON
Eight Dead In Vicious Shooting
Doone Gang Head For Border

Eight men were gunned down in the Montana cattle town of Lasserton this week when the notorious Doone gang held up the North Country Bank and got away with a haul reckoned to be close on $10,000.

Reports reaching here yesterday put the gang within five miles of the North Dakota border at Big Bend on the south-eastern trail heading for Remark . . .

"CHESTER Woodley!" bellowed Sheriff Jim Brent, throwing open the door to the print-shop and offices of *The Remark Bugle* and banging it shut again with an angry thud. "Chester Woodley — this time yuh gone too far! Too far by a mile, and I ain't havin' it! No way am I havin' it. Chester, yuh hearin' me?"

The sheriff's cold breath swirled in clouds around his head; the snow on his thick fur coat and heavy boots began to melt and drip to dark puddles on the office floor. He ran a cold hand over the crisp stubble at his chin and narrowed his gaze on the gloomy, half-lit depths of the room.

"Chester!" he roared again. "Where in tarnation — "

"Darn it, Sheriff, don't yuh ever leave a fella to his work?" came the voice from somewhere hidden. "Bustin' in here like a bull in a barn of heifers . . . Can't yuh see I'm workin', darn it?"

"I can't see nothin' of yuh, dammit!

Yuh just get out here, will yuh, and tell me how it is yuh fillin' this rag-bag newspaper of yours with fool stories about the Doones ridin' for Remark. I ain't never read nothin' so brain-scattered crazy in m' life. Never. Now just get out here!"

Sheriff Brent grunted, sighed, blew into his hands and gazed round the dusty office with its softly smoking stove, drunken piles of papers, scatterings of books, dusters, cloths, bottles of ink, glasses and, lurking like a sleeping beast in the darkest corner, the ancient printing press. His gaze moved to the smudged window and the empty street beyond it where the already deep snow suckled eagerly at the flurry of a new fall.

"Chester, I ain't got all day!"

"Me neither," said the voice at his back as Chester Woodley wiped his hands on an ink-stained cloth, cleaned his cracked glasses, adjusted his eyeshade to the top of his balding head and blinked his tired but still twinkling blue eyes on the light from the window. "What's yuh problem?" he asked, rummaging in the folds of his apron for the butt of a half-smoked cigar and matches.

"Problem," croaked Brent. "Problem, f'crissake! M' problem, Chester, is this newspaper of yours. No, that ain't quite so. M' problem is the darn fool writin' it and printin' it. You, Chester, you're the problem!"

"That so?" murmured Chester, lighting the cigar and blowing a slow curl of smoke. "How come?"

Brent sighed and reached to the table nearest him for a copy of the week's edition of the *Bugle*. "This," he said, slapping a hand across the headline story.

Chester replaced his glasses and peered at the front page. "Yeah," he said, quietly. "Yeah, I see that. So?"

"So what's it mean, f'crissake?" fumed Brent.

"It means the Doone gang raided the

bank at Lasserton, grabbed around ten thousand or so and rode hell-bent for Big Bend headin' this way. Yuh can read, can't yuh?"

"Don't get smart, Chester. Yuh know darn well what I'm sayin'." The sheriff threw the paper aside. "Yuh know as well as I do that talk of the Doones makin' for Remark is enough to set the town hummin' with panic. Yuh know them scum, know the trouble they bring. Liquorin' up, wild shootin', mebbe killin', takin' the women . . . There ain't no holdin' them. Never has been, not when they were in the territory all them years back, and not since they been plaguin' the West like poisoned hornets. If they hit Remark . . . " Brent eased his hat from his brow. "Talk like you're puttin' about is scare-mongerin' rumour, Chester, and that's the truth of it. And yuh ain't got no evidence f'sayin' it. Not a shred."

"How'd yuh know I ain't?" asked Chester. "Who's sayin' I ain't?"

"I'm sayin' yuh ain't, darn yuh!" snapped Brent. "Big Bend is close on thirty miles away. Thirty miles of the roughest country this side of Little Falls. Thirty miles right now of deep snow, freezin' winds, frozen trails . . . Why, I heard only this mornin', not an hour ago, as how the train due here t'night will be the last outa Big Bend fer mebbe ten days. That's how tight the winter's gripped. I don't figure the Doones ridin' in on no train, and I sure as hell don't reckon on them hittin' the trail. I'll tell yuh what they'll do: they'll hole-up at Big Bend til the weather eases, then swing south fer Wyomin'. That's what they'll do, sure as hell."

Chester blew another cloud of smoke. "T'ain't the way I hear it."

Brent sighed again. "Stubborn as a fool mule, ain't yuh? Anyhow, how come yuh hearin' things outa Big Bend that I ain't — *if* yuh are?"

"Well, now," began Chester, examining the glow of his cigar. "I'll tell yuh.

Telegraph — yuh know, a wire down the line from Big Bend to Remark. That's how I'm hearin', Jim. Telegraph. But I ain't sayin' who's wirin' me. That's m' own business, and stayin' that way."

Sheriff Brent's eyes narrowed. "Yuh mean yuh got somebody back there at Big Bend who's keepin' yuh informed?"

"Precisely," grinned Chester. "Sorta underground. Known in the business as a contact."

Brent stood silent for a moment. "He reliable?" he asked.

"As day to night. Know'd him from way back. He don't make mistakes."

"And yuh ain't sayin' who?"

"Nope."

Brent shifted uneasily. "Even so," he muttered, as if talking to himself, "don't say as how he's right. Things change."

"True," said Chester, blowing more smoke, "but I wouldn't lay money on this fella bein' wrong."

There was a sudden stomping of

boots on the boardwalk beyond the office, a sneeze, a cough, then the door opened and the snow-soaked youth in his crumpled railroad uniform and over-size cap stumbled into the room.

"Sorry — " he began, and sneezed again.

"Yuh should get somethin' for that cold, Luke," said Chester, leading the youth to the smoking stove. "Catch yuh death this time of year. Yuh got somethin' for me, boy?"

"Sure thing," spluttered the youth, fumbling in his trousers pockets. "Wired outa Big Bend just a half-hour back. Came straight here minute I got it." He glanced nervously at the sheriff. "Mornin', sir," he smiled thinly, handing a slip of paper to Chester.

Brent simply nodded and grunted.

"Well, well," murmured Chester, scanning the wire. "Well, well." He raised his tired eyes to the sheriff. "Yuh'd best read this, Jim. Real careful . . ."

Big Bend: 10.28 a.m. To Chester Woodley. The Remark Bugle, Remark. Message reads: No change of plan. Gang leaves noon. Southeast trail. Signed: S.

2

"GENTLEMEN of the town committee ain't goin' to take kindly to this, Sheriff, and no mistake. Not at all kindly. T'ain't in the nature or proud civic thinkin' of the gentlemen to react so to printed talk set to frit. Nossir. Fact is, Chester Woodley needs bringin' clean to heel. Time he had a lesson or two in responsibility."

Isaiah Raithe shrugged his scrawny shoulders under his long frock coat and glared at Sheriff Brent through his brown hawkish eyes set close at the top of a beaky nose. His thin lips tightened and he looked, thought Brent, watching him, just exactly what he was: a shrewd but always mean-minded storekeeper who doubtless kept the candy jar locked in the safe overnight.

"Responsibility, I say," continued

Raithe. "Lord above knows — and praise be t' Him too — I can remember the time when this beloved town of Remark was no more than dirt-clingin' shacks fated to Hell, rotten to the core, and full of yellow-bellied critters at that. Well, we sure turned it round. Yessir! Turned it. Cleared the scum. Built the town. Made it. Gave it character, Mister Brent, the character of survival, and best of all courage — fearless, unyielding courage. So what yuh goin' to do, Sheriff? That's what the gentlemen want to know. What yuh goin' to do?"

"Ain't a deal I can do right now, Mr Raithe," said Brent, carefully. "I ain't got much to work on."

Raithe sniffed. "Seems to us — the gentlemen, that is — that Chester Woodley is either hopelessly wrong in his printed presumptions — in which case he needs horse-whippin' and his newspaper closin' down — or frighteningly right. And if he's right, we, or more correctly *you*, should be actin'. Fast. If them Doones get within five miles of Remark, we got real trouble."

"Chester's right, up to a point," said Brent. "But only to a point. The gang's set to ride, sure enough, and this way. But that don't mean they got Remark in mind."

Raithe sniffed again. "Ain't a deal between Big Bend and Remark, and nothin' after. So . . . " The man's claw-like fingers picked at the pile on his coat. "This wire yuh seen reliable?"

"Reckon so. But I don't know who sent it, and Chester ain't sayin'."

Raithe's eyes glinted. "Doubtless he can be persuaded," he grinned. "Meanwhile . . . yes, meanwhile, the gentlemen will meet t'night back of my place. Be there." He adjusted his coat. "How long we got?"

Brent leaned back in his chair and gazed at the window overlooking the street from his office. "No tellin', not in this weather." He watched the flurries of soft snow settle on the panes.

"Two days, mebbe three. Can't say for certain. Last train from Big Bend is due here t'night. I reckon the engineer will have the best report on what conditions are like for travellin'. He'll know if the trail is open fit for ridin'. I'll see him." His gaze shifted back to Raithe. "I don't want any panic in town, Mr Raithe. Yuh understand? No panic."

"That may not be so easy," said Raithe, turning to the door. "I hear as how the *Bugle*'s sold clean out. Not a copy t' be had nowhere."

★ ★ ★

Irene Patch — more popularly known to all in Remark as Sugar — swung her long shapely legs from the bed in her room at the Boundless Saloon, tossed her auburn hair into her neck and wrapped her nakedness in the snug closeness of a blanket.

Even so, she shivered as she padded to the door and picked up the copy of the *Bugle* that somebody had slid beneath it. Must have been young Slim, she thought, or maybe Walt, perhaps young Joey, or could be that nice man from the bank, Mister Grant. Any one of a dozen or more. Who cared? They were all the same.

She flung the newspaper on the bed and padded to the window. Still snowing. Hell, she hated winter! Hated the grey days, the long nights, but most of all the cold. The cold was no comfort in her business. But how come it never seemed to bother men?

She sighed and shivered again as she watched Isaiah Raithe cross the street to his store. The Lord save her from another visit from him. He was just snake-slithering crude . . . But maybe something would come up to keep him occupied with the gentlemen of the town committee. A slow grin broke across her lips. Gentlemen be darned!

Sugar turned, tossed the tresses of her hair again and gazed over the scattering of clothes littering the room. Time to clear up, get dressed, face the dreary world and the cold-fingered men. She frowned as her gaze settled on the headlines on the *Bugle*'s front page. Could that be, she began to wonder as she crossed to the bed. Was that . . . ?

The blanket had slid from Sugar's body by the time she had read the report, and now she was shivering uncontrollably.

"Not him," she murmured, her blue eyes darkening. "Not Malachy Doone."

★ ★ ★

Doc Maloney packed his medicine bag carefully, checked and rechecked the contents, then turned from the table in the back parlour of his home and walked to the window.

He watched the snowfall swirling on the drift of the freshening wind, shifted his gaze higher to where there should have been sky. Now there was nothing save the grey blanket of leaden winter cloud, the few listless smudges of light already fading in the early afternoon. Night would come early, he reckoned. Early and hellishly cold. No time for a man to be out on the trail. But he had no choice. Sam Baker's problem would hardly wait for the weather.

He sighed, put his back to the window and reached for his hat. Maybe he was getting too old for doctoring. Maybe he should retire, take life easy, find himself some place out California way, a place in the sun — leaving the treating of patients in mid-winter to somebody younger. He sighed again, knowing full well that he would be here, in this room, packing this bag, come the spring, just as he always had been. There were a dozen more Sam Bakers always waiting . . .

The doc shrugged himself into his fur coat, picked up his bag, took a last look round the room and left the house for the livery where Ridge Parker would have his mount waiting. Hell, it was cold, he thought, as he crossed the street.

"No time t' be takin' to the trail," called Ridge as he brought the doc's horse from the stabling. "Must be a deal urgent."

"It's Sam Baker," said the doc, rubbing his hands together over the glowing forge. "Gotta change the dressin' on that leg of his. Can't afford t' leave it."

"Hell, Doc, Sam's place is a good ten miles away. Some distance in this weather."

"Don't remind me!" grinned the doc. He patted the mount's neck. "She up to it, yuh reckon?"

"Fit 'n fresh," said Ridge. "Like I've always said, Doc, yuh gotta darn fine horse here. One of the best I've ever clapped eyes on." He stroked the mare's neck affectionately. "We gotta soft spot fer each other, me and her. Ain't that so, gal?" The mare snorted. "Yeah, a real soft spot. Wouldn't ever wanna see her put t' bad use, so yuh go easy with her, OK? She ain't no more fussed with the cold than y'self."

"I will, I will," said the doc, mounting and turning the mare to the open street.

"Sooner you than me," murmured Ridge as he watched Doc Maloney disappear into the swirling snowfall on the trail heading west for Big Bend.

3

SHERIFF JIM BRENT gazed round the room at the back of Isaiah Raithe's general store and wondered why it was that the shadows lurking there beyond the dim lantern light were gathered like some dark premonition. Maybe they too felt the threat of the Doones. Maybe they could already see what was coming.

He sighed and leaned against the pile of dusty blankets, thankful to be out of the cold draughts that fingered the cracks of the old wooden walls, and let his gaze move to the faces hanging like masks in the gloom.

Fat Lou Fletcher, hairdresser and proprietor of the town's cleanest bathhouse; suave Reet Morgan, owner of the Boundless Saloon; grey Adam Thyme, undertaker; Ridge Parker, blacksmith; Charles B. Grant, banker; and Isaiah

Raithe — the gentlemen of the Remark Town Committee. All of them sweating in spite of the cold.

Raithe cleared his throat importantly. "I ain't goin' t' go through the report I reckon we've all read in the *Bugle*," he began to murmurs of agreement. "Seems like there's a mite of truth in it, accordin' to Sheriff Brent here." He paused, watching the faces. "Chester Woodley ain't givin' a deal away as yet, but I figure that's his affair for the time bein'. Point is — "

"Point is," interrupted Grant curtly, "what are we goin' to do if the gang hits town?"

"That's it precisely," said Morgan, examining his fingernails.

"Well, I fer one — " began Fletcher.

"Hold it!" snapped Raithe. "Let's keep it cool. Let's consider."

The grey undertaker dabbed a soft handkerchief at his lips. "Yuh can't hurry hands of fate," he murmured for no reason and to no one in particular.

"If the Doones are clear of Lasserton

and holed-up at Big Bend," Raithe went on, "then they got options: they could stay holed-up against the weather and turn south when it improves; they could head north and trail the Montana border; they could, on the other hand — "

"Cross it," said the sheriff quietly from the shadows.

"Explain that, mister," said Grant.

Brent eased away from the pile of blankets. "Seems t' me they ain't goin' t' be keen to hang around Montana territory. That won't be Jubal Doone's thinkin'. He'll wanna bring the gang across the border and find somewhere far enough away from Lasserton and safe enough for mebbe a week to plan his next move. Weather's against him, but also for him. No posse's goin' t' get further than Big Bend, and by the time they do, Doone'll wanna be provisioned up, refreshed, ridin' new mounts and clear to head where he wants."

"Courtesy of Remark," sneered Morgan.

"My livery," said Parker.

"My bank, darn it!" croaked Grant.

"We can't allow that, Sheriff," gestured Fletcher. "No way can we allow that."

The undertaker shrugged and dabbed his lips.

"Which brings us to a point of resolvin' matters," called Raithe above the hubbub. He waited for the gathering to fall silent. "Looks t' me as if we're goin' t' have to put ourselves, and the town, in the hands of the law. In the hands, gentlemen, of our worthy sheriff here."

"Agreed," clipped Grant.

"Same here," said Morgan.

"And here," echoed Parker and Fletcher.

The undertaker smiled softly.

Sheriff Brent settled his hat and smoothed the fingers of his right hand across the butt of his holstered Colt. "Thanks for the vote of confidence," he grinned, then paused, narrowed his eyes as the grin slid away on tight lips, and drawled, "Now let's face facts."

He stepped from the shadows to the pool of lantern light. "It's a whiles since the Doone gang were houndin' Dakota territory, and never close enough to Remark to ruffle yuh ways, so most of yuh — mebbe all of yuh — ain't never set eyes on the Doones, let alone crossed them. I have."

Parker and Fletcher swallowed noisily. Grant coughed. Reet Morgan raised his eyes. Raithe adjusted his coat, and the undertaker dabbed.

"Jubal Doone still heads up the gang," continued Brent. "He's gettin' old now, but age ain't changed a mite of his character. He's still as mean as ever. Still a killer with no second thought for who he's killin' or why. He just don't give a damn. And he's raised his two boys, Malachy and Caleb, in the same mould, savin' that they're worse. Odd one out of the four is Jubal's daughter, Celebration. She's the youngest, fathered late, somewhere east of Fargo. Jubal thinks a lot of her, dotes on her, spoils her — but don't go gettin' the wrong idea about her just 'cos she's a woman. She's got a pretty face and the body of an angel, but she kills as easy as the others, and laughs loud when it's done."

Sheriff Brent paused again, searching the faces watching him. The sweat on them was beginning to glisten. "The Doones take what they want where they find it, and if that means rapin', killin' and lootin' fer it, that's all part of the entertainment. Nobody argues, not if they wanna stay alive."

"All very interestin', Sheriff," said Grant, "but the law — "

"The law ain't never got within spittin' distance of the Doones," snapped Brent. "Nearest they've ever come is t' feel hot lead in the gut. Jubal boasts four sheriffs and a marshal to his credit. The others ain't much fer countin'."

"So what yuh advisin'?" asked Raithe, quietly.

"If the Doones hit Remark, I'm goin' to need deputies. Good, reliable men who don't scare easy. Mebbe a half-dozen. Who's volunteerin'?"

Nobody moved, nobody spoke.

Brent shrugged. "Says a deal for the town committee, don't it?" he drawled.

"Now hold on there," urged Fletcher. "There's men in this town who'll help, sure there is. Gotta be."

"Then yuh'd best get to roundin' them up," said Brent.

"Mebbe we should call in some guns," said Grant.

"From where?" asked the blacksmith. "It'd take days for men t' get here in this weather."

"Mebbe we all need a drink," said Morgan.

"The last supper . . ." murmured the undertaker.

"Enough!" announced Raithe, raising his arms. "Let's simmer it down and think straight. I propose the sheriff draws up a plan and we act on it. Darn it, he is the law round here."

"I second that," said Grant.

"All agreed?" asked Raithe.

The gathering grunted its approval.

Brent sighed. "I'll do the best I can. Can't say more."

"'The Lord is my shepherd . . .'" began the undertaker, crossing to the room's dark window and peering through it. "Ground must be frozen real solid out there. My, my, ain't that goin' t' be a problem . . ."

4

FOUR riders, black as night, muffled in heavy coats and the blankets of their bedrolls against the swirling snowfall, cleared the border into the territory of North Dakota in the gloom of the late afternoon, and did so without pausing or exchanging a word between them.

Their mounts snorted, steamed and struggled through the bitter, wind-whipped cold and fought for every foothold in the snow. Their eyes flashed wild fear, but they responded instantly to their riders' firm hold on the reins and knew better, it seemed, than to deny their masters.

The leading rider sat his mount like a hunchbacked crow, indifferent to the weather and the treacherous going, but his gaze ahead into the gathering darkness was razored, sharp as a knife-edge, missing nothing, seeing everything, piercingly cold and grey without a flicker of emotion. The straggling tufts of his shoulder-length white hair danced on the wind like ghostly fingers so that he appeared to move over the land as if summoned from it by some haunting whisper of command. This man was Jubal Doone.

Close behind him was his son, Malachy, who followed in his father's tracks as he always had without question, anxious only that shelter and warmth should be close and this nightmare journey done with. He had no stomach for winter, still less for being forced to ride into the grip of it. And he knew, as well as the man ahead of him, that time was running out for the woman whose mount stumbled through the snow at his side.

His sister, Celebration, had been hit real bad back there in Lasserton; a loose, lucky shot, but she was still bleeding, growing weaker, her body slumped, her eyes dim and misted, a trickle of saliva dripping constantly from her lips. She would be hard-pushed to stay mounted another half-hour.

The fourth rider was Caleb Doone, the only one of the family to have spoken in the last ten miles of miserable trailing. He had wanted to know where they were heading, to what, and when they would get there. Did anybody have any idea "'cos I'm sick with this cold and darned snow." But no one had answered him. No one ever did. He guessed they would have to trust to Pa as ever. Pa always knew, always did the right thing as he saw it, his way, in his time, no arguing, specially when it came to Celebration.

Spoiled brat! Not for the first time that day, Caleb wished they had never set eyes on Lasserton. Nothing had gone right since then . . .

Jubal Doone trailed the party another three miles before he veered gently south-east towards what he was now certain was a twisting curl of smoke on the darkening backdrop of the winter light.

A homestead, for sure, he figured; remote and lonely behind the drift of a ridge. But someone was living there, had a fire, warmth, food and hot coffee, and a bed for the girl. Hell, she needed a bed more than anything, somewhere to rest and sleep. She also needed a doc, and fast. That would not be so easy, but maybe his luck would hold.

"Yuh see that, Pa?" called Caleb. "Yuh see that smoke? We headin' fer it?"

"I see it, boy," croaked Jubal.

"Must be folk livin' there."

"That figures," sighed Jubal.

"Reckon so, Pa. We sure need t' hole-up fer a while. Celebration here ain't goin' to make it much further. Seems t' me — "

"Will yuh shut yuh mouth, Caleb!" drawled Malachy. "Just leave it to Pa, right?"

"Right!" snapped Caleb, and spat fiercely.

There were lights in the two small windows of the homestead, bright yellow lights that glowed like eyes in the snow-swamped huddle of the building and seemed for a moment to stare defiantly at the four riders, daring them to move closer. Jubal Doone stared back and waited for a movement, listened for a sound. There was nothing. He grunted and urged his mount forward.

The four had come to within a few feet of the homestead's veranda when the door opened and a woman, snuggling into the shawls at her shoulders, stood in the pool of light.

"Oh," she gasped, gazing hurriedly over the shapes and shadowed faces before her. "I heard a horse. Thought it was Doc Maloney. I'm expectin' him. M' man's sick."

Jubal Doone stared hard at the woman. For all her distress, the biting cold of the wind that whipped round her, she was good-looking, sure enough, with deep-blue eyes, a pert nose, full, inviting lips, corn-coloured hair, and a body, he guessed, that no man would turn his back on. He grunted again and held his mount steady.

"Sorry to hear of yuh troubles, ma'am, specially in weather like this," he murmured, the stare still fixed and steady, "but we gotta young gal here who's sure in need of lookin' to. She's my daughter, ma'am, and I'd be real obliged if we could get her indoors and into bed."

The woman pulled at the shawls and shivered. "I only got the one bed, mister, and m' man's in that. I couldn't think of movin' him, but yuh'd be welcome t' use the parlour. I gotta good blaze goin' in the hearth."

"Only one bed," muttered Doone. "Yeah . . . well, now, I guess I'm goin' to have to insist on takin' that, ma'am. Like I said, this is m' daughter here, and I set a whole lot by her well-bein'."

The woman frowned and stepped back. "But yuh can't," she began. "M' man's real sick."

"Malachy," ordered Doone gruffly, "see to it, will yuh? Get that bed sorted fer yuh sister."

"No!" the woman protested, easing into the doorway. "Yuh can't!"

But Malachy Doone had already dismounted, a pinched grin playing at his lips, and thudded on to the veranda. He pushed the woman aside and strode into the home, slamming the door shut behind him.

"This won't take a minute, ma'am," drawled Jubal. "Then we can all get int' the warm."

The woman's eyes flashed in panic, glazed with sudden fear. She turned to the door, had her hand on the latch, when the roar of the gunshot split the night and the snowfall swirled on a gust of wind. The mounts bucked. The woman screamed.

"Shut her mouth, Caleb," snapped Doone. "Any way yuh like."

5

CHESTER WOODLEY slid his cracked spectacles to the tip of his nose and stared at the clock on the wall of the *Bugle* print-shop. Still another three hours to go before the train from Big Bend arrived at Remark, always assuming, he thought, with a grunt, that the track was still open. Could be that the snow had closed in real tight; could be that there was too much ice. No telling what might be happening up the line.

"Heck," he groaned, wiping his ink-stained hands on his apron as he turned to the windows overlooking the street. "Sonofabitch weather!"

He watched the snowfall dancing like swarms of white flies in the glow of the lights. Few folk about, he reflected. Hardly the night for taking a stroll. But maybe it was not just the night, the cold and the snow that were keeping folk indoors. Maybe they had other thoughts, other fears.

Maybe they too were watching clocks and wondering when the Doones would ride into town.

He was about to turn back to his workbench when a shape at the batwing doors of the saloon caught his eye. Now what in tarnation was Sugar doing outdoors at this time of night? And heading this way at that.

Chester had the door to the printshop open as the woman reached the boardwalk and stood dusting the snow from her cape.

"Mr Woodley," she smiled. "I was kinda wonderin' — "

"Come in, come in," said Chester, taking Sugar by the arm. "Nothin' to be said fer hangin' about in this weather."

"Like I was sayin', I was kinda wonderin' . . . " the woman paused and bit nervously at her bottom lip. "I ain't sure this is the right thing t' do," she began again. "But I just gotta tell somebody, and it seemed right — yuh bein' the one who started all the talkin' ... I ain't makin' no sort of a job of this, am I?"

"Yuh in some sorta trouble or somethin'?" asked Chester.

"Not yet," frowned Sugar. "But I sure don't think it's far away!"

Chester closed the shop door and led the woman to the warmth of the stove. "Somethin' I can help with?" he queried.

Sugar gazed for a moment into the old man's tired eyes where, even in this light, there was a reassuring twinkle. "It's about them Doone critters," she said. "I read your report this mornin' and figure that mebbe yuh right: mebbe them scum will head for Remark. In fact, I'd guarantee it."

Chester eyed the woman carefully. "Yuh seem t' be speakin' with some authority, ma'am."

"I am," said Sugar tightly. "First-hand experience of all of them — Jubal,

Malachy, Caleb, and that bitch, Celebration. I know 'em all, and they know me."

"Tell me," said Chester patiently.

The woman stared at the stove as if summoning some dark memories. "It's more than three years back now," she began, "long before I turned up here in Remark. At that time, I was workin' a place west of here — the Silver Belt at Benswood. Same line of business. I ain't apologizin' fer that. Anyhow, the Doones hit the town like a whirlwind come one fall, and Malachy, who's got a real hankerin' fer women, took an unhealthy shine t' me, so much so that when the gang decided t' ride out he insisted on takin' me with them." Sugar paused, looked at Chester, then settled her stare on the stove again. "They held me fer close on six months — a half-year of hell. Wasn't 'til the spring that one night when they were all liquored up I managed to slip away and hide out in the hills 'til they tired of lookin' fer me. But I know Malachy,

Mr Woodley, know him only too well. He won't have taken kindly t' me gettin' free of him like I did. It'll fester in him like a sore, and when he finally gets t' me . . ."

"But he don't know yuh here, does he?" said Chester.

"Guess not. I drifted around fer a while before fetchin' up in Remark, but Malachy Doone don't f'get a thing, specially where women are concerned." Sugar shifted her stare to the old man. "I ain't makin' no bones of it, mister, I'm scared clean through. I can't run, not in this weather, and if I stay . . . Minute Malachy sets eyes on me . . ."

"Hold on," said Chester, laying a hand on the woman's arm. "Don't get to panickin'. There ain't no good goin' t' come of that." He considered for a moment. "Seein' as how yuh've shared a confidence, mebbe I can share one with you." He considered again, then lifted his gaze to the clock on the wall. "Last train from Big Bend is due here around midnight. There's a man on board that train who might just be the answer t' the Doones."

"One man?" frowned Sugar. "It's goin' to take a darn sight more than one man to settle them scum!"

"But that," smiled Chester, "depends on the man, doesn't it?"

"Who is he?" asked the woman.

Chester Woodley's smile broadened. "Friend of mine. Fella by the name of Stryde."

★ ★ ★

Young Luke Banners yawned, stretched, rubbed his knuckles into his sleepy eyes and shivered. Rail station telegraph office sure was one hell of a cold place to be at midnight in the middle of a gripping winter, he thought, coming to his feet and crossing to the faint warmth of the stove. Still, another few minutes . . . He glanced at the clock. Five past midnight. No telling, of course, if the train would be anything like to time.

Could be all manner of problems up the line.

Luke reached for his jacket, slid into it, then primed and lit a lantern and went to the door.

The freezing wind clawed like some beast set to devour him. The snowfall continued to swirl on the backdrop of the black night. He stood for a moment shivering, the lantern raised, and watched the shadows leap around him. Hell, he would be glad to be home and snug between blankets on this Godforsaken night, and no mistake.

The whistle of the train when it came over the darkness was like some long, forlorn cry from the wilderness, but the sound of it lifted Luke's heart. "Here she comes," he murmured through icy breath, and smiled to himself in spite of the cold. "Sonofabitch, she made it!"

Soon there were other sounds: the heave and hiss of racing pistons, the clang and clatter of wheels on steel, the throbbing chug as the great machine rolled on. And then the headlamp, piercing the night like a staring eye, the sudden wind-tossed curls of steam, a fountain of sparks from the footplate, lost like fiery midges on the darkness.

Luke raised the lantern above his head and waved it wildly.

Only one passenger stepped down at Remark; a tall, easy-moving man, hat pulled tight down on his head so that you saw nothing of his face or the chipped ice gleam in his eyes. The wind caught at his long coat, lifting the folds, then settling them to the bulge of the .45 at his waist.

The man stared at Luke for a moment, unmoving, unaware of the whip of the wind, the biting cold, then nodded and turned without a sound to the night and the snowfall that swallowed him instantly.

"Heck," mouthed Luke, his eyes still wide on the space where the man had been, "who in tarnation was that?"

6

DOC MALONEY reined the mare to a halt, blinked, and stared ahead at the soft glimmer of light. He could be wrong . . . perhaps he was seeing things . . . maybe he had been on the trail too long, was too cold and wind-addled to make any sense of anything. But hell, no, he thought, that *is* a light.

He urged the mare forward again and brought her round through the darkness and snowfall to an outcrop of rocks and beyond them the stiff fingers of pines. Now he was sure. This was Sam Baker's place clear enough. Just looked a mite different in this weather!

He brushed the snow from his face and patted the mount's neck. Shelter, warmth, something to eat and drink . . . The thought of the prospect brought a soft grin to his lips. Maybe a portion or two of Lori Baker's beef and potato pie . . . now there was a prospect!

★ ★ ★

Doc Maloney's instinct only half told him that something was wrong. It could have been the silence as he approached the Bakers' homestead. It could have been the absence of any response to the snorts of the mount. It might have been the aura of tension that seemed to surround the place, as if it waited, holding its breath. More likely it was the bitter-sweet smell of tobacco that reached him on the cold night air as he dismounted and moved to the door.

Sam Baker had never smoked.

The doc paused, his hand raised to knock, sniffed and had part turned to the soft movement to his left, when the man in the shadows stepped forward.

"That's far enough, mister."

The words were ground out of a

deep throat like broken rock. Doc saw the glint of a Colt barrel, the gleam of wild eyes, teeth clamped on a cigar, then the twisted lips in a gritty, unshaven face, stained lean shape of the man in his ragged clothes as he took another step forward.

Malachy Doone — Doc had seen the features on a hundred posters.

"Yuh the doc?" croaked the man.

"Doc Maloney. I'm here t' see — "

"I know what yuh here for. I heard. But yuh ain't wanted on that count. Fella's dead."

Doc moved, halted at the thrust of the barrel. "Dead? He can't be. I was — "

"Dead I said, dead I mean," snapped Doone, his eyes flashing. "I should know. I killed him."

A colder, tighter chill slid across the doc's shoulders. "Yuh did what?" he murmured.

"Killed him. Shot him. Pa said as how we needed his bed. So now we got it." Doone spat the cigar butt clear of his mouth and grinned. "Fella's out back, but he ain't feelin' the cold none!" He giggled wheezily. "Inside," he drawled, motioning with the Colt.

Doc Maloney blinked as he stepped into the smoke-hazed room of the homestead where only a single lantern glowed on the littered table. He was conscious of a second man leaning against the wall by the tired smoulderings of a fire, of a soft sobbing somewhere in the depths of the shadows, and then of the sudden scrape of a chair pushed back and the looming, crow-hunched bulk of a third man — a man with long white hair straggling from beneath his black hat, grey sullen eyes and aged, sallow skin stretched tight over a bone-filled face.

"And about time too," the man grunted. "Folk could get to dyin' waitin' on a physician."

"You who I think yuh are?" croaked the doc. "Jubal Doone?"

"S'right," sneered Doone, leaning across the table to stare directly into the doc's eyes. "Yuh just been greeted by m'son, Malachy. Over there's m' second son, Caleb. M'daughter, Celebration's in the back room. And that snivellin' wretch down there in the dark is a woman I ain't got round to askin' fer a name. M' boys've been a deal more interested in her other assets. Satisfied?"

Doc Maloney felt the sting of the sweat in his neck, the surge of blood as his anger grew. He made to move away from the table, but stiffened at the prod of Malachy Doone's Colt between his shoulders. "If you've touched Mrs Baker . . . " he seethed. "And what about Sam? Yuh killed him? Just like yuh did those folk back at Lasserton. I heard about that too. In God's name . . . "

"Oh, f'Crissake simmer down, will yuh!" groaned Doone, pulling the chair back to the table and sitting down. "Yuh tirin' me, mister. Yuh hear that, tirin' me? It's been a long day and it ain't done yet. Fact is, there ain't no point in yuh rantin', is there? Yuh do as I say from here on." He wiped his mouth with the back of his hand. "That fella, Baker, was dyin', anyhow. Could see it plain enough, and I seen plenty. As fer his woman . . . she's a woman, ain't she?" A nerve in Doone's shallow cheek twitched as if a bone had turned over. "I got more pressin' matters to attend to."

"Yuh'll get nothin' from me," snapped doc. "Nothin'!"

Doone sighed. "Oh, my, I might've known. We got a man of principles. Should've figured as much, yuh bein' a doc." His scrawny fingers tapped menacingly on the table. "Well, t'aint so much of a problem." He raised his sullen eyes. "M'daughter's in need of medical care back there — and yuh're goin' to see to her, Doc. Right now."

"Yuh can go to hell!" flared Doc.

"No, mister, I ain't goin' no place, and neither are you. But if yuh don't show a deal of co-operation, we can sure make it difficult fer this Baker woman." Doone's grin was slow and wet. "M'boys are good at that. Hungry and very demandin'. They don't leave a deal worth the clearin' up."

Doc Maloney stiffened. "I'll see yuh hang for this, so help me God," he croaked.

"That's as mebbe. Just get t' tendin' m'daughter, will yuh? And just so's yuh don't go gettin' thoughts about not doin' yuh duty, keep this in mind." Doone gestured to the man leaning on the wall by the fire. "Get her," he ordered.

It took the full support of Caleb Doone's arms and firm grip to keep Lori Baker on her feet. Her head rolled on her shoulders as if in the trauma of fever. Her hair was sweat-soaked across her bare shoulders, the few strips of clothing covering her body hanging like chewed rags. She was a bruised, battered, bewildered and almost lifeless shell of the woman Doc Maloney had known since that day all those years back when she had arrived in the territory as fresh as new spring. And now her once bright eyes were staring into winter nightmare.

"She's alive, Doc, and she could stay that way," murmured Jubal Doone, hunching his crow-black shoulders. "But that, o'course, is up t' you."

7

THE lights went out in Remark after midnight, but the brooding silence of the town, the emptiness, the snowfall drifting through the darkness, suited Sheriff Jim Brent just fine. In these dead hours he had the town to himself. Almost.

There was another body on the move this night, and that intrusion did not suit, not one mite.

Brent had waited in the shadows by the rail station until the last train out of Big Bend had pulled away from Remark with a shuddering spin of wheels, and watched the tall stranger who had left it disappear into the night. There was no hurry to follow, he had reckoned. The man's tracks wherever he was heading would be clear enough. He was content for the moment to wait for Luke Banners to douse the lantern in his office and reflect on what the engineer had told him.

"Yuh too darn right, Sheriff," the man had said when Brent had climbed to the glowing footplate, "them Doone critters were back there in Big Bend leastways close by — but I heard reliable enough that they crossed the border trailin' your way." The man had wiped his sweating face on an oily rag. "Hard t' tell how far they're goin' to get. Trail's tight and fillin' in, but passable right now. I wouldn't put it past them scum to make it through to here. Their kinda luck, ain't it? Still . . . " He had eyed the sheriff closely. "I also heard tell as how that daughter of Doone's took a hit in the raid. Bad wound, they say. Reckon that could slow the rats down."

Sheriff Brent grunted to himself, stamped some warmth into his cold feet, and turned from the shadows as the light went out in Luke Banners' office.

Doone's daughter wounded, he

pondered; how bad — bad enough to force Jubal to change his plans? But to what? He would do most anything for that daughter of his. Brent grunted again and turned his attention to the stranger's tracks.

The man, whoever he was, had moved quickly and directly to the main street. No attempt to slink about like some wily coyote. Had he already fixed on where he was staying, who he was meeting? Chester Woodley?

Not Chester Woodley, thought Brent, as the tracks passed the *Bugle* frontage and headed on. Maybe the saloon, or perhaps Ma Bailey's rooming-house.

Brent halted, peered ahead and blinked the snowfall from his lashes. Hell, the tracks were making straight for his own office!

★ ★ ★

The sheriff's office was dark, silent and seemingly deserted, save for the footsteps through the snow that ended at the covered boardwalk fronting it.

Brent came closer, peered and eased his coat aside to clear the holstered Colt. His fingers drummed lightly on the butt, then settled, tightened, and began to lift the gun from leather. He took a step forward, eyes narrowed now, squinting for the shape he was sure was there, ears primed for the slightest sound.

"No need for that, Sheriff," drawled the soft, deep voice from the darkness to the left of the door. "Ain't no trouble hereabouts."

"Who are yuh? What yuh want?" asked Brent, slipping the Colt to rest. "Yuh lookin' for me?"

"Could say that, or mebbe you're lookin' for me." The man stepped into the pale light. "Name's Stryde, but I guess that won't mean a thing. Don't matter none right now. We got other things t' discuss."

"Such as?"

"Such as them Doones and how yuh

goin' to handle them when they hit this town."

Brent stiffened. "I'm the law round here, mister, and I handle things as I want them handled." His gaze narrowed again. "Anyhow, how come yuh know they're headin' this way? And how come — "

The man spat into the snow and turned his piercingly blue eyes into Brent's. "Reckon yuh might not have tangled that close with this bunch before. T'ain't a pretty sight." A wispy grin flitted across his face. "Yuh'd best be ready, Sheriff. Real ready." The man lifted his gaze to the empty street. "Time I turned in. Been a long day. We'll talk again. T'morrow. Early." And then he walked away.

"Hey, hold it, mister," said Brent. "Just a minute. I wanna know . . ." But the man was already walking on. "Where yuh stayin'? Where yuh from? Who in tarnation are yuh?"

"T'morrow," called Stryde, without looking back.

★ ★ ★

Other pairs of eyes were watching the tall stranger as he made his way through the snowswept main street of Remark on the bleak winter's night.

Isaiah Raithe followed the man through cold, hooded eyes from the dark windows of his store. A stranger who had arrived on that last train out of Big Bend, who walked straight and tall and confident, who looked dark and fearless, who was, thought Raithe, undoubtedly a gunman. But who, he wondered, had sent for him? Jim Brent, Chester Woodley? Maybe more to the point, how much was he going to cost the town, and who was paying?

Fat Lou Fletcher had been restless for hours. Sleep had been no more than cat-napping, and even his dozes filled with grim images of blood and bodies. Now, as he watched the man in the street from his bedroom window, he shivered and pondered how it was that a fellow would want to be about at this hour, in this weather, and where, damn it, was he heading? Looked from here as if he knew. Looked from here, in fact, as if this man knew a whole lot of things. Most of them of the dangerous kind.

Remark's undertaker rarely felt the cold. Death and dead bodies had left Adam Thyme immune to its bite, but he was a light sleeper and had woken instantly at the sound of the train's whistle as it clanged into town. Now he too viewed the man in the street with close interest.

You could tell a killer straight off, he reckoned. They had a cold presence, same as this fellow; a slow, steady walk, measured out as if walking into destiny. And always that haunted stare through icy-blue eyes. He would wager that this fellow had blue eyes when, and if, you ever got to see them.

But for Sugar at the window of her room in the Boundless Saloon, the man in the street was a welcome sight. So he had made it, just as Chester had said he would. Good for him, thought the woman. She just hoped his luck would hold out, for all their sakes.

Sugar stayed at the window until the man had crossed to the offices of the *Bugle* and disappeared inside, then she turned back to the bed where Reet Morgan waited for her.

"Hey, what's fascinatin' yuh so?" he asked, turning aside the blankets. "Yuh watchin' out for ghosts or somethin'?"

She smiled the same inviting but meaningless smile she always smiled on these occasions, and slipped out of her clothes.

"No," she murmured, "just makin' sure the right one's here."

8

DOC MALONEY wondered how long it would be before sleep finally swamped him — and then if he would ever wake again. He sighed, came to his feet from the chair at the side of the bed, and stared at the young woman motionless beneath the blankets. Maybe he should be asking himself if she would ever wake again, he thought, and bent closer to the sleeping form.

Celebration Doone's gunshot wound was bad, as bad as they came, and the bullet was still in there. Getting it out was going to be a long job, and difficult. Chances were she would not survive it. Fact was, she maybe had no right to survive. Could be, thought Doc, it would be kinder to let her die where she lay.

He wiped a sudden break of sweat

from his brow. Emotion was getting in the way of doctoring. He was letting his anger at the cold-blooded shooting of Sam Baker and the abuse of his wife stifle his medical commitment; stepping into the dark world of revenge.

He came upright with a start. He would do his best by Celebration Doone; of course he would. He was not in the business of taking life.

The door at his back opened and Jubal Doone's shadow fell across the floor. "How's she doin'?" he asked. "She goin' t' be all right?"

"Like yuh see, she's sleepin'," said the doc, without turning to face the man. "I've done m' best f' now, but that wound's bad, mister, and I can't get to clearin' it here. I need to operate, and I'd need to tackle that at m' own place."

Doone grunted. "Yuh foolin' me, Doc? 'Cus if yuh are — "

Doc Maloney swung round, his face taut, eyes fierce with anger. "Unlike you, Mister Doone, I don't fool around with life!" he flared. "I'm in the business of keepin' folk from pain and misery and as far from death as I can manage. Don't go thinkin' any other, or f'gettin' it." He stiffened. "This woman needs the sort of attention and treatment I can't give her here. I ain't equipped to even try. I could only do that back at Remark. But I'll do by her meantime as I would anyone else. There ain't no more t' be said."

Jubal Doone leaned on the door jamb and stared long and hard at the doc as if stripping the very flesh from his bones. "Yuh speak yuh mind, Doc," he said almost softly. "I like a man who speaks his mind, and I believe what yuh tellin' me, but that daughter of mine is goin' t' live, come what may, whatever the cost. So we'll take her to Remark."

"What!" flared Doc again. "That distance, in this weather? She'll never make it. Hell, man, she couldn't even sit a horse!"

"She won't have to," said Doone, pushing himself away from the jamb. "There's an old buckboard out back. Horses with it. We'll load her onto that, comfortable as we can make her."

"But — " began Doc.

"No arguin'," snapped Doone. "We leave at first light."

He had half-turned when he added, "And I'll keep t' my side of the bargain. The Baker woman comes with us — alive. That suit yuh?"

★ ★ ★

Ridge Parker's efforts to sleep through that night to the cold early hours and the first hint of a dawn coming up had been a waste of time.

How was he expected to sleep when his mind tossed and turned with thoughts of the doc and the mare out there in this Godforsaken freezing weather? How could a man get to relaxing when all he could think of was a frozen trail, swirling snow, the mare fighting for every foothold, exhausting herself, growing colder, weaker . . .

"Hell!" he had finally cursed, throwing aside the bedclothes and struggling into his pants. "This ain't no time at all t' be sleepin'. Time t' be doin'!"

It had taken Ridge only minutes to dress in his warmest clothes, light a lantern in the livery and begin saddling up a mount. He knew the trail to Sam Baker's place well enough, but what he might find on it was another matter. There was no telling in these conditions. "Fool doc should've stayed put," he murmured to himself. "Right where he was."

A half-hour later, Ridge had cleared the still sleeping and silent town and turned into the lick of wind on the western trail. The snowfall had eased a mite, but the clouds were thick and heavy with the threat of more to come. Full daybreak would be slow to make it, he reckoned. And who could blame it?

★ ★ ★

Chester Woodley watched the man seated opposite him in the back room of the *Bugle* offices finish his last mouthful of steak, take a gulp of his coffee, and relax in his chair.

"She hurt bad?" asked Chester, easing forward to the table.

Stryde's blue eyes were suddenly sharp and focused. "Can't be sure," he said. "She was hit, that's for certain. Took the shot just as the gang were clearin' Lasserton. Plenty enough witnesses to that. But as t' how bad . . . " The man drummed his fingers on the table. "She's a Doone. That means she's tough."

Chester's old eyes narrowed behind his cracked spectacles. "Fact is, though, she's goin' to slow them down, ain't she? But yuh know Jubal, he won't prejudice that girl, not for nothin'. He'll stick with her, get her to a doc — " Chester thumped a fist on the table. "O' course, a doc! Should've realized. Only doc within strikin' distance is right here in Remark. Our own Doc Maloney. Hell! Best get to warnin' him."

Stryde came to his feet and crossed to the window where the first of the morning light was struggling for a hold. "Him and a whole lot more," he murmured. "Town's goin' to have to stand t'gether if it wants t' come outa this still breathin'." He paused and sighed. "We been through this before, Chester," he went on. "Same sorta town, same sorta folk livin' in it. And the Doones ain't changed one bit. Remember Carsway?"

"Like it was yesterday," answered Chester.

Stryde ran his fingers over the cold windowpane. "One sonofabitch day that was. Blood, lead, dead and dyin' . . . and still the Doones rode free. I ain't f'gotten one minute of it. Not one second."

"Know somethin'?" said Chester. "I recall Carsway for somethin' a whole lot more agreeable. That's where we first met, ten years back. Yuh remember? You the southern marshal sittin' on the Doones' tail; me headin' north with a crazed dream of foundin' a newspaper. Helluva lot of dust blown up since then."

"And not all of it settled," murmured Stryde. The man turned from the window. "We both gotten older, Chester, but there's a difference."

Chester peered over his spectacles. "Oh, how's that?"

"Looks t' me as if yuh found yuh dream. Yuh got yuh newspaper. But I ain't got the Doones." The blue of the man's eyes turned colder. "Could be this is goin' t' be m' last chance."

"Mebbe," said Chester. "But in my business, friend, there's always two sides to the story." He smiled softly. "Could be it's goin' t' be the last chance for Jubal Doone. Let me tell yuh about a woman, name of Sugar. She could be useful . . ."

9

DOC MALONEY peered through the curtain of unbroken grey light and turned the collar of his coat higher into his neck against the icy wind. The cold of that bleak morning was eating into him like a creeping pain, working its way through limbs, joints and muscles until it seemed they were no longer a part of him and numbed beyond recall. It was as much as he could manage now to sit astride the mare and keep her nose pointed to the snow-capped trail.

The buckboard, handled by Malachy Doone, slithered, rolled and bumped ahead of him as if held in the grip of an ice-licked sea. God knows, he thought, what each turn of the wheels, every heave of the struggling team to find a foothold, was doing to Celebration Doone and Lori Baker. They simply lay side by side, wrapped in blankets, their eyes closed, faces expressionless, unaware perhaps of where they were or who they were, conscious only of the faint, anonymous warmth generated between them. It would be a miracle, he reckoned, if either made it to Remark.

Jubal Doone held his mount close to the side of the buckboard, his eyes flitting constantly to the women, the trail ahead, where Caleb rode point, then swinging to a wider gaze over the surrounding country. He stayed silent, a dark haunting through the snow and wind, but missed nothing.

Doc pulled at his collar again, tipped the brim of his hat lower, and pondered the prospects. Not good, he decided, not even if they had the luck to make it to Remark. Seemed clear enough now what Jubal had in mind: he would hold Doc and Lori Baker hostage against any action the town might reckon it would take. His only concern would be for his daughter, and when — more likely if — she recovered, he would shoot and kill his way out Doone-style in whatever direction he fancied.

Doc grunted. No easy prospect for Sheriff Brent and whatever so-called deputies the gentlemen of the town committee might drum up. No time either for him to summon outside help in these conditions. He grunted again. Chester Woodley would have a deal of head scratching over his next *Bugle* headline!

But supposing, he pondered, just supposing there was something could be done now, here on the trail, before they reached Remark. Not a deal, he reckoned, not one man against three; not if he wanted to stay alive and not end up like Sam Baker in a cold snow grave. He shivered at the thought of Sam, of Lori. "Dammit!" he mouthed, and felt a sudden warmth in his anger.

Only consolation he had, he figured, was that Jubal Doone needed him alive. No doc would almost certainly mean no daughter. Maybe that was the ace Doone had been forced to hand him. Jubal's problem would be that he would never know when Doc might choose to play it . . .

★ ★ ★

It was close on an hour later, with the morning light still grey and vague and flurries of snow dancing on the wind, when Caleb Doone raised an arm to halt the party then turned his mount and rode back to Jubal.

"Rider up ahead," he grunted. "Comin' this way."

"Know him?" asked Jubal.

"Nope, and he don't look t' be no lawman."

"He alone?"

"Seems so."

Jubal turned to the doc. "Yuh expectin' company?"

Doc Maloney smiled softly. "Sure — half the cavalry!"

Jubal spat into the wind. "I ain't in no mood fer humour, mister. Cut it."

"T'ain't right t' be hangin' about like this," called Malachy, impatiently. "Too darned cold, and there's snow pilin' up fast. Best do somethin'."

Jubal stared long and hard at Caleb, then spat again. "Do it," he drawled. "No messin'."

Caleb simply nodded.

"Hold it," said Doc, urging his mount forward. "What yuh plannin', f'Crissake? Fella's mebbe just passin' through. He ain't no threat to yuh."

"I'll be the judge of that," snapped Jubal. "Keep outa this, Doc. T'ain't your business."

"The hell it is!" croaked Doc. "Yuh can't — "

But Caleb had already turned again at the snort of a mount on the trail and the sight of the hunched, dark figure of the rider as he moved towards them, one hand shielding his eyes against the snowfall.

"Hey, there!" shouted the man. "That you, Doc? How yuh doin'? Yuh get through t' Sam? Hell, there sure is one almighty snowfall back there."

"Ridge Parker," murmured Doc, staring at the man. "What in tarnation . . . ?"

"I reckoned on yuh mebbe needin' some help," called the man again. "How's the mare? She OK? Didn't figure on yuh — "

And then Caleb Doone's Colt spat through the morning like a vicious lick of flame, the first shot hitting Ridge Parker clean in his chest, the second toppling him from the saddle as if no more than a dead branch broken on the wind.

"In God's name!" yelled Doc.

Caleb Doone fired again, this time from close range as Ridge twitched into death throes in the snow, his fingers clawing at the frozen ground. "Doc . . . " he hissed. "Doc . . . " he hissed. "Doc . . . " The shot blazed into Ridge's forehead. He moaned, twitched again, and lay still, snowflakes settling like white blossoms on his staring eyes.

Doc Maloney sat his mount stunned and motionless for a moment, his body suddenly drained, his mind a blank, empty space. "Yuh bastard!" he mouthed. "Yuh sonofabitch bastard!" He settled a cold, unblinking gaze on Jubal Doone's face. "I'll see yuh die for this, so help me God I will."

Doone spat and grinned. "Seems like the fella knew yuh. He from Remark?"

"The livery," muttered Doc. "Thought a lot of the mare."

Doone shrugged. "He's done with worryin'." He called to Caleb. "Load the body on the horse. We'll take him in. Fair warnin' of what happens when yuh cross the Doones."

"Yuh'll die, Doone, yuh'll surely die," muttered Doc again. "And God willin', I'll have the pleasure!"

"Mebbe, mebbe," said Doone, dismissively, then turned at the sound of a groan from the buckboard. "Look to my daughter, Doc. Now!"

The Doc did not move. "Go t' hell!" he hissed.

Doone smiled. The wind caught at the strands of his long white hair, scurrying them over his bony cheeks like the fingers of death. "Yuh want fer me to finish the Baker woman?" he grunted. "'Cos make no mistake, mister, I will. I surely will."

Doc shuddered at the sting of the wind.

"So save y'self a whole heap of remorse and get to my girl," grinned Doone. "Then we'll all go home to Remark."

Doc waited another moment before easing his mount to the buckboard. "It'll be like ridin' into Hell," he drawled as he passed Doone. "And there won't be no ridin' out for yuh. Never."

Jubal Doone stared at the Doc's back and for the first time that day felt the icy closeness of the cold, as if the wind had suddenly found him.

10

"THEY'RE comin'! My God, they're comin'! Large as life and twice as ugly! Can yuh beat that f' arrogance?" Lou Fletcher turned to the others gathered outside the livery at Remark and waited for their response to the sight in the far distance on the trail west that riveted their stares. "Well, f'Crissake, somebody say somethin'!"

Isaiah Raithe cleared his throat but stayed silent. Reet Morgan pulled nervously at the collar of his coat. The undertaker began to hum a hymn. Charles B. Grant murmured "Hell!" and buried his hands in his pockets. Chester Woodley squinted through his cracked spectacles and said, "Looks a deal like a dead body on that horse they're trailin'. A dead body f' sure." Sheriff Jim Brent took a step forward. "And that's Doc Maloney ridin' alongside the buckboard," he grunted.

"We have a problem, Sheriff," said Raithe.

"A brilliant piece of observation, mister!" snapped Grant.

"What the hell's goin' on?" spluttered Fletcher. "Has anybody got any idea?"

"Sure," said Morgan, "the Doones are ridin' into town with Doc as their prisoner."

"How in tarnation did he get involved with them scum?" croaked Fletcher.

"Must've ridden out t' take a look at Sam Baker," murmured the undertaker. "Sam ain't been well fer months."

"So who's in the buckboard, f'Crissake?" asked Grant.

"Must be Doone's daughter," said Brent. "Talk is she took a hit back at Lasserton."

"And that trailed mount is Ridge Parker's horse," added the undertaker. "Mebbe that's Ridge slung across it. Looks t' be about his size. But where's

Sam and Mrs Baker? They back of the buckboard too?"

The others glanced at Thyme as he began to hum again and sway gently to and fro, then turned their stares back to the trail, the snowy waste and the dark group moving ever closer across it.

"What's yuh plan, Sheriff?" asked Grant quietly. "What yuh goin' to do?"

"There ain't no plan," grunted Brent.

"Yuh just goin' to let them ride in?" said Fletcher in a voice beginning to squeak.

"Sure is," said Morgan, lighting a cigar. "He don't have no choice, does he? Not unless we wanna fill the street with dead bodies."

The undertaker's humming rose a pitch.

"Will yuh cut that morbid wailin'!" snapped Grant.

"We must wait," said Chester Woodley. "We gotta hear what they have to say."

"There'll be no bargainin'," said Raithe. "We don't bargain with murderers and rapists."

Reet Morgan blew a line of smoke to the freezing air. "That remains t' be seen," he grinned.

"I said no — " began Raithe again.

"That's enough!" clipped Brent. "Chester's right, we wait. We hear what they gotta say. Meantime . . ." He glanced round him. "Anybody seen that stranger who hit town last night?"

"What stranger?" asked Grant. "I ain't seen no stranger."

"I seen him," said Raithe. "Saw him in the street. Gunslinger if ever I saw one."

"Gunslinger?" frowned Fletcher. "Where'd he drift in from?"

"Big Bend. Last train," said Chester Woodley. "And he ain't no gunslinger."

"Yuh mean yuh know him?" asked Morgan.

Chester shrugged and adjusted his spectacles. "Sort of."

"So where is he?"

"He's about — somewhere," said Chester, blandly.

"Never mind," snapped Brent. "There ain't the time for findin' out. We got other business — closin' in like bad weather."

They fell silent and went back to watching the trail.

★ ★ ★

Jubal Doone waited until he was just out of gunshot range before reining his mount and calling the party to a halt.

"Stay close, mister," he croaked, turning to Doc Maloney. "Caleb, yuh keep a close eye on them critters up ahead. One move to a gun, and yuh let that Winchester of yours talk real lead. Malachy, yuh hold that buckboard steady. Yuh don't move, none of yuh, 'til I say so. Got it?"

The two sons grunted their understanding.

"Yuh ain't goin' to get away with this Doone," said Doc. "No town's goin' to just stand back t' yuh like that. There ain't a man livin' — "

"Shut yuh mouth, Doc," snarled Doone. "I'm doin' the talkin' round here."

He urged his mount forward a pace or two, halted, then sat tall and straight in the saddle, his white hair flowing on the wind, his stare steady, face grey and unflinching to the scattering of icy snowflakes. "Now hear this," he called in a voice that cut across the air like sudden flames. "Yuh all know who I am, I guess, and yuh know m'boys here too. Ain't had the pleasure of meetin' none of you, but that's a situation we're goin' to change. We're comin' into town and there ain't any single one of yuh goin' to lift a finger t' stop us. Yuh hear that? Good. Now, I got yuh doc here who's goin' to look to m'daughter who ain't feelin' none too good. I also got a Mrs Baker. She kinda got herself widowed, but she's alive. Back of me, slung across his horse, is some fella from yuh livery. He ain't takin' no interest in things any more. That's on account of him bein' stiff dead."

Doone paused a moment. "So, like I say, we're comin' in and stayin' fer as long as it suits. I ain't lookin' fer no trouble, but if any of yuh should get to playin' the hero, I can assure yuh that the Baker woman will die, then Doc. No heroes. OK? If there are, they'll all be dead ones." He paused again. "Right, we're startin' in." He turned to Malachy. "Move it, son. Doc, yuh point the way straight to your place. No messin'."

Doc Maloney shuddered under a new surge of anger. "Left at the saloon," he murmured.

★ ★ ★

"It ain't for real," mouthed Grant, drily.

"Oh, but it is," said Reet Morgan, blowing a new line of cigar smoke. "Real as day, Mister Grant. Real as day."

"We just goin' to stand here?" asked Fletcher. "We just goin' to let the sonsofbitches in after what they done to Sam Baker and Ridge?"

"Don't none of yuh move," said Sheriff Brent. "Not if yuh wanna stay breathin'."

"But we can't just — " croaked Fletcher.

"We can!" snapped Brent. "They'll gun Lori Baker soon as spit on her."

"Oh, my," sighed the undertaker.

"They sure as hell look as mean as folk tell," said Chester Woodley, adjusting his spectacles. "None meaner, I'd reckon."

"Animals!" hissed Grant. "Nothin' better than animals."

"With very sharp claws!" said Morgan. "So don't tangle."

"We'll need to reconsider our position, Sheriff," said Isaiah Raithe, brushing the snow from his coat. "Very, very carefully."

Brent flashed the man an impatient glance. "Yuh can say that again."

"There'll be a meetin', my place. Early evenin'," added Raithe. "Yuh'll all be there."

"Or them still alive," crawled Morgan.

"Oh, my. Oh, my," sighed the undertaker, and began to hum again across the drift of the thin wind.

★ ★ ★

And so it was on that bleak winter's day that the Doones rode unchallenged into Remark. They passed slowly down the main street, turned left at the saloon and finally brought the buckboard to a creaking halt outside the home and surgery of Doc Maloney. Their progress was watched in silence by fearful faces and frightened stares from behind darkened windows. No one, it seemed, dared to voice their nightmare thoughts. Only one man watched from the darkest shadows with a glint in his eyes. For him, the best was still to come.

11

SHERIFF JIM BRENT helped himself to another coffee from the pot on the stove in his office and held the warm mug close in his hands. His stare went far beyond the window, the flurries of snow, the empty street in the grip of winter. His thoughts were a turmoil of what to do, how and when to make his next move.

Maybe he would try getting a team of men together to tackle the Doones, stage an onslaught of blazing lead on the doc's place until they were all dead, at whatever the cost. Maybe he should somehow burn the place to the ground. Would anyone count the bodies as long as the Doones were among them?

He shivered and sipped at the coffee.

Or maybe he should walk out of here alone and do what a man who carried a badge was supposed to do. Gentlemen of the town committee would like that, if they lived long enough to get to chewing it over. Or maybe . . .

He turned at the creak of a floorboard behind him and peered into the gloomy rear of the office.

"Back was open," said the tall dark shape of the man in the shadows. "Reckoned it was time we talked."

"We got somethin' to talk about?" asked Brent, setting aside the coffee.

"We could start with the Doones and how you're goin' to handle things from here on."

"*You* could start, mister, by tellin' me who yuh are, where yuh come from and what you're doin' here."

The man stayed in the gloom. "Name's Stryde, like I told yuh. Ain't from no place in particular, savin' any place that happens t' be where the Doones are creepin' outa the woodwork. I gotta real hate of them. That do yuh?"

Brent walked to the window and

gazed over the gathering late afternoon dusk. "Glad t' hear yuh on my side," he said. "But that don't make yuh no law round here. That's my piece of the action. So when it comes to handlin' the Doones — " He paused suddenly, stepped closer to the window, and rubbed his fingers over the top pane. "Sonofabitch!" he croaked. "If that don't take some beatin'! Yuh seen this, mister? Malachy Doone ridin' down the street like he owned the place! Did yuh ever — "

But when he turned, the gloom at the back of the office was empty.

★ ★ ★

Reet Morgan watched the approaching rider through narrowed eyes and a soft curl of cigar smoke. Got to hand it to the Doones, he thought, they sure had arrogant style. Take this one, Malachy, sitting that mount like he was some big land baron looking over his spread; straight-backed, easy hands, no hurry;

carrying side arms, Winchester in its scabbard.

Morgan blew another curl of smoke and crossed to the batwings of the saloon. One good shot from a high window would drop the fellow like melting snow. Just one good shot . . .

But no man in Remark would fire it, not while the Doones held Doc Maloney and Lori Baker. They would rate their deaths too high a price to pay — for now. Time might come, though, when compassion gave way to fear and panic . . .

Meantime, Malachy Doone was heading straight for the saloon. Fellow obviously needed a drink, and maybe more.

Reet Morgan turned and called into the bar. "Hey, Sugar, get y'self out here, will yuh?"

* * *

Malachy Doone reached the saloon, halted, waited, his eyes moving carefully round him, then dismounted slowly, hitched his mount and crossed to the batwings. He gazed over the doors into the long reach of the bar where no more than a dozen customers lounged with their drinks, blew smoke, and were silent now, watching the man as he slid his fingers from his gloves as if releasing wild animals from their cages.

Charles B. Grant, seated at a table at the far end of the bar, raised his glass of whiskey to his lips and finished the measure in one angry gulp. "Scum!" he mouthed, his eyes fixed on Doone. "Nothin' else for it. Scum!"

He rested his arms on the table. Fellow worth his salt would gun the sonofabitch right now, he thought. No messing. Just gun him. World would be a better place, and banks a deal safer! If he were twenty years younger . . . He poured himself another drink. Where the hell was Sheriff Brent?

"House's open, Mister Doone," smiled Reet Morgan from the other side of the batwings. "Step inside. What's yuh pleasure? This one's on me."

Doone parted the batwings and walked to the bar.

"Whiskey, I'll bet," said Morgan at his side. "Yuh look like a man who knows his whiskey. That right? Well, so happens we got the best in the territory hereabouts. Yessir, finest there is." He clicked his fingers at the open-mouthed barman. "A bottle of the best here." He turned to the others. "Drinks on the house, boys. State yuh preference."

Charles Grant pushed back his chair, came defiantly to his feet and crossed the room. "I wouldn't be seen dead drinkin' with scum like that!" His eyes flashed as the colour rose in his already florid cheeks. "I ain't one for mixin' with animals! Can't stand the smell!" He shot Doone a fiery glance.

"Now, now," soothed Morgan. "Ain't no cause to go gettin' ourselves all lathered up, is there?"

"Every reason," snapped Grant. "And yuh're no better, Reet Morgan. Soft-talkin' that sonofabitch!"

There was not a man in the bar who did not blink and feel his heart pound at the speed of Malachy Doone's sudden movement. In one moment he had a glass to his lips, in the next there was a Colt in his hand as he stood back and released a vicious blaze of lead that hit Grant square in the chest.

The banker stood perfectly still for a few silent seconds, his eyes wide in a glazed stare of shock and surprise, mouth open, arms loose at his sides. Blood bubbled from his chest, soaking his fancy waistcoat, dripping to the floor like soft rain. His fingers fluttered as if to stem the flow, and then his body shook through a shuddering spasm of trapped breath, and he fell back, scattering chairs and a table as his bulk thudded to the boards. He did not move again.

"F'Crissake," murmured someone.

"Hell," croaked another.

"Charlie never carried a gun . . . "

Reet Morgan dropped his cigar. A glass slid out of the barman's fingers and shattered at his feet.

"Who was he?" asked Doone, standing at the bar again and pouring himself a drink.

"Charlie Grant. Banker," spluttered Morgan.

"Ain't never shot a banker that close before," grinned Doone. "He should've kept his mouth shut."

Heads turned as the batwings swung open and Sheriff Brent stepped into the bar, his breath curling from his mouth like mist. "What the hell — " he began, then glanced at the body and stared at Doone.

"Keep yuh hands clear of yuh guns, Sheriff," drawled Doone. "This place is beginnin' to get a mite too busy."

"Yuh'll hang for this, Doone," murmured Brent. "And I'll be the first — "

But that was as far as Brent went. The movement on the stairs to the upper rooms of the saloon had drawn all eyes, holding them like bright stones fixed in ice.

Doone lowered his glass to the bar, pushed it aside, and narrowed his gaze. "Well, now," he said slowly. "Just look at that, will yuh . . . Ain't this my day? Never thought I'd set eyes on yuh again, Sugar, but I sure as hell ain't complainin'. Nossir!"

The woman paused and stared at him, her eyes cold as if seeing a ghost, her face white and blank as that dead winter's snow.

12

IT took what seemed to those gathered there like an age for Sugar to reach the foot of the stairs. No one moved, no one spoke. Even the stiffening body of Charles B. Grant lay unnoticed as if no more than a part of the furniture. All eyes were on the woman, and hers on Malachy Doone who watched her with a fixed, consuming leer that seemed to summon a thousand memories.

"Go back, gal. Get the hell outa here," said Brent. "This ain't no place for you."

"Not so fast, Sheriff," snapped Doone. "This lady and me are kinda acquainted. Ain't that so, Sugar? Yuh tell the fella."

The woman shivered but her stare remained firm. "We were when yuh took me," she murmured. "Not any more we aren't."

"Aw, come on now," grinned Doone. "That ain't so. Sure, yuh may've given me the slip, but, hell, before that . . . Shall I tell them, Sugar? Shall I tell them all about those things we got up to? Sure would make colourful listenin', eh?"

"That's enough," clipped Brent. "We ain't interested. Sugar, do as I say and get your butt outa here. As for this — "

Doone's sudden blaze of lead ripped into the back of the bar like a tornado, shattering bottles, glasses, mirrors. Slivers of glass flew in all directions; timbers splintered; smoke hung like a shroud.

"Don't yuh go givin' orders, lawman," roared Doone, waving his Colt across the cowering bodies. "I'm callin' all the shots here. OK? Don't go f'gettin' it, unless yuh wanna deal more blood splashed over this floor." He glared round the faces. "Now, stand back, all of yuh. Right back. Clear the way for the lady. She's comin' with me."

"*I don't reckon so.*"

The voice drifted from somewhere at the shadowed top of the stairs, a keen, levelled voice with an edge that cut across the thickening air of the saloon like a blade and hung in a long echo.

Faces lifted, eyes explored the gloom. Only the woman stared ahead, watching Doone, the softest flicker of a grin at her lips.

"Who's sayin' so?" said Doone, his eyes darting over the shadows like bats. "Who's up there?"

"*Don't matter none.*" The voice drifted again, this time from a different area.

Doone fired wild and blind, his eyes narrowed, probing the higher darkness. Sheriff Brent, Morgan and the others in the bar backed away, Brent wondering if there might be the chance . . . Then changing his mind when Doone's stare settled on him in a menacing threat. Sugar stayed where she was, almost relaxed, waiting, watching, the soft grin still playing at her lips.

"Show y'self, yuh sonofabitch," called Doone.

This time there was no reply. A silence settled as if balanced on the brink of the darkness. Doone wiped a line of sweat from his brow and turned his concentration on the woman.

"Come here," he ordered. "Now!"

Sugar hesitated a moment, glanced hurriedly round her, fingered the folds of her skirt nervously.

"I said now!" cracked Doone.

"*Stay where yuh are, ma'am.*"

Now the voice was far to Doone's right. His eyes flicked to where he thought it had a body, his lips tightening angrily. "Goddammit, show y'self," he yelled.

The silence settled again. Sugar remained at the foot of the stairs. Brent's fingers itched to reach for his gun. He knew that voice. He had heard it only a half-hour ago in his office.

"Have it your way, mister," called

Doone. "I'm leavin'. Yuh hear me, leavin'?"

He turned from the shattered bar and began to edge towards the saloon doors, his eyes still fixed on the shadows at the top of the stairs, his Colt raised and levelled for the movement that never came.

"I'll be back for yuh," he murmured to Sugar. "Yuh can count on it."

Doone had his back to the batwings and was within a dozen shuffling steps of reaching them, when he stopped, froze, a frown creasing his forehead, his eyes glinting. There had been a noise, a creak, somewhere out there on the boardwalk. A footstep. That sonofabitch critter must have . . .

Doone spun round, gun tight in his hand, eyes wild and yellow in the half light of that winter's day.

The man he faced for those few seconds stood tall and straight on the other side of the batwings; a dark, silhouetted figure, faceless, silent; a shape that seemed to have simply materialized. Doone saw nothing of the man's eyes, nothing of the tautness in his face, the set of his lips — but he was aware of the batwings opening and the glint of a Winchester barrel slanting between them like a snake.

And he surely heard, as if swamped by a shuddering earthquake, the rifle's roar, saw the blaze, then felt the rush of pain in his gut, the sickening spread of it as it went deeper until he was consumed by it.

Soon the darkness rolled in to leave only the sparkle of distant snowflakes fading on his dying stare.

There was no more of Malachy Doone.

★ ★ ★

It was left to the grey-faced, softly humming undertaker and one of the bewildered saloon bar customers to load the bodies of Doone and Grant on to a buckboard.

"Take them back to your place,"

said Sheriff Brent. "We'll get t' buryin' them soon as we can. And make sure yuh go real slow when yuh pass Doc Maloney's. Mebbe somebody'll be takin' note."

"Mebbe somebody'll be fired up for revenge," said Reet Morgan, lighting a fresh cigar. "This ain't goin' to do nothin' to make Jubal Doone's day."

"We'll see," answered Brent.

Morgan blew smoke. "Who was that fella did the shootin'?" he asked to murmurs of agreement from the others gathered on the boardwalk. "I ain't seen nothin' like that hereabouts before. And where the hell did he go?"

"Perhaps we should leave that 'til later," said Isaiah Raithe softly. "These are solemn times. We have lost Ridge, Sam, and now Mr Grant."

"But we got one of them Doone critters!" clipped one of the customers.

"At a price, sir. At a price," murmured Raithe.

"Grant should've sat quiet," said Morgan. "He should never have riled

Doone like that."

"Too late now," said Raithe. "Let's get inside. There's a young lady in there we gotta thank fer her courage . . ."

"And I gotta bar in there lookin' like the far side of Hell!" muttered Morgan. "Who's goin' t' pay fer that?"

Chester Woodley waited on the boardwalk until it had cleared before making his last entry in his notebook and slipping it back to his pocket. Some day, he reflected, some day . . . Maybe there would have to be a special edition of the *Bugle* at this rate.

He glanced anxiously through the scattering of snowflakes to the still heavy sky. Night would close in real fast, he reckoned. That would suit Stryde for what he had in mind.

Pity that nobody knew what Jubal Doone might be thinking.

13

"SONOFA-crack-brained-bitch! I might've known he'd go windin' up trouble for himself. Never could keep his head, save when somebody was protectin' it." Jubal Doone crashed a fist on the table and set a long, sinewy nerve in his bony cheek twitching violently. "Should've sent yuh with him, Caleb. That's what I should've done. Ain't thinkin' straight."

Doone lifted his tired eyes to his son seated opposite him in the doc's back parlour. "Whoever it was shot him . . ." he murmured.

Caleb Doone leaned forward. "Let's finish that Baker woman and throw her to the street dogs," he hissed. "Then let me go get a couple of them town scum and make a real mess of them. Let me do it, Pa, for Malachy. He'd have gone along with that. He'd want us to do it, don't yuh reckon?"

"Sure he would," said Jubal, "and that's mebbe just what them boneheads out there wants us to do. But I ain't playin' no games to their rules. It's our rules, son, our rules."

"But Pa — " began Caleb.

"Mind's made up," snapped Jubal. Then he grinned. "But I ain't goin' to spoil all yuh fun. I gotta little somethin' I want yuh to do come dark. Somethin' to churn them townsfolks' stomachs! Meantime, go get the doc."

Caleb Doone was smiling as he left the room, but Jubal's grin had faded in the grey shroud of his thoughts. Just who, he wondered, had been fast enough and smart enough to gun down Malachy? *Who* in a town like Remark?

His fingers drummed darkly on the table. He had the cold feeling that a ghost was watching him.

★ ★ ★

"Well," said Isaiah Raithe, "what now?" He paused in his measured steps round the dimly lit back room of his store and stared hard at Sheriff Brent. "Doone will almost certainly avenge the death of his son. But when, and how? Will it be Lori Baker, the doc? You? Me?" He flicked at the dust on his coat. "We mebbe don't have a deal of time, Sheriff."

Brent shrugged and crossed to the flickering glow of the lantern. "Never no tellin' with the Doones," he said, watching the glow. "We just wait."

"And trust that the stranger will come to our rescue once again?" grunted Raithe.

Brent stiffened. "I ain't sure . . ." he began.

Raithe waved a hand dismissively. "Nobody's gettin' at yuh personally, Jim, but they are askin' questions, and rightly so. Who is this fella? Where'd he come from? Where does he disappear to?" He eyed the sheriff coldly. "Whoever he is, he ain't here solely for the benefit of Remark. He's here to kill the Doones. Ain't that so?"

Brent coughed lightly. "Mebbe, but he ain't no gunslinger, and he ain't no bounty hunter neither. I'd swear to that."

"Might be an idea if we asked the fella face to face. Why not go find him, bring him here? Let's get to talkin' with him while there's still enough of us left to talk." Raithe's face darkened. "Mebbe he's our only way outa this mess."

★ ★ ★

Lou Fletcher had heard a noise. A sound he did not recognize or understand; one that had lifted a sticky sweat on his brow and forced him to retreat to the deepest shadows of his locked, bolted and empty barber's shop.

It was no day noise. No night noise, come to that. It was the sort of noise you waited for, wondering if it was closer, or fading. A somebody noise or something noise, wondered Lou, wiping his brow? It was no stray hound, that was for sure. No loose board caught in the wind. No creaking door or window. So it had to be somebody.

He swallowed and wiped his sweating hands down his sides. There it was again . . . Over there now, somewhere towards the back of the shop. Moving, pausing, waiting. Maybe it was also watching.

"Who's there?" he called, peering into the darkness.

Maybe he should light a lantern, get to real grips with whatever it was. Darn it, this was his property! Nobody had the right, or reason at this hour, to go trespassing.

Lou stepped from the shadows to the table at his right, laid a hand on the lantern and fumbled for a match. "Never got one to hand when yuh need it," he muttered.

Thirty seconds later the lantern glow

fingered the gloom and pushed back the shadows, but for Lou Fletcher there was still nothing to see, to explain the noise he had heard. "Don't make no kinda sense," he muttered again, lifting the lantern. "Must be hearin' things . . ."

But Lou had not been hearing things, not by a long shot, but he never saw who had made the noise as he took the vicious blow on the back of his head and felt his senses spin into a fiery whirl.

He was face-down on the floor in a pool of his own blood when the man stepped over his body, collected the lantern and tossed it casually into a mound of sheets and towels.

Caleb Doone smiled as he watched the flames take hold and begin to spread. Fire sure had a way of settling things, he thought. All down to ashes . . .

He waited another ten seconds, glanced quickly at the unmoving body, then slid away to the winter darkness.

He reckoned Remark was in for a warm night!

* * *

"Hell!" yelled Sheriff Brent as he rushed from his office to the street and headed for the inferno blazing at the far end of it. "F'Crissake, it's Lou's place! Where is he?"

Reet Morgan and a dozen or so customers tumbled through the batwings of the Boundless Saloon. "Sonofabitch!" shouted Morgan. "Who the hell — ?"

"The Lord spare us," muttered Isaiah Raithe as he slipped into his long coat, locked the door to his store, then double-checked that he had, and padded into the snow.

"Oh, my. Oh, my . . ." chanted the undertaker as he followed Raithe, clutching his Bible in one hand and his order book in the other.

Chester Woodley threw aside his eye-shade, shoved his worn hat on his head and struggled into his heavy winter coat. "Man don't get to spendin' time for his own breathin' these days," he chuntered. "If it ain't one thing, it's sure as fate another." And then he too rushed into the street and joined the throng facing the blaze.

"We're too late," shouted Morgan, shielding his eyes against the glare. "Place is too far gone."

"Where's Lou?" yelled Brent.

"He ain't out here, that's fer sure," retorted someone.

"Can't we get in there?" called Raithe.

"No chance," snapped Brent as a shower of sparks and flying slivers of timber lit the night sky. "Roof's goin'."

"Sonofabitch!" mouthed Morgan.

"Oh, my," chanted the undertaker.

"We gotta save the town," roared Raithe. "Don't let the goddamn flames spread! Yuh hear me?"

Heads turned at the sudden crack and blaze of gunfire at the opposite end of the street. Eyes peered and probed the night, looked beyond the shadows cast in the glow of the fire, widened and narrowed for shapes they could recognize.

"It's the Doones!" shouted Morgan. "They're saddled up and ridin' out!"

The throng edged a few paces forward. Eyes widened again, faces glistened, wet with sweat; mouths opened at the sight of Jubal Doone astride his mount, a Colt blazing wildly into the darkness from his right hand. Caleb Doone's Winchester roared once, twice, three times, shattering the street ice, lifting the snow in dancing flurries.

"T'hell with the lot of yuh!" yelled Jubal. "T'hell with yuh town! T'hell!"

Then he lifted the mount high on its hindlegs, let rip another round of shots, brought the horse to its four feet, turned and rode into the night like a spectre, Caleb and a third rider following.

The throng watched, silent, unmoving, as if frozen into the slush of the street, the flames of the barber's shop still licking at the darkness.

"They gone?" asked the undertaker. "Just like that — gone?"

"Seems so," murmured Morgan.

Sheriff Brent swung round with the others at the swish and slosh of hooves from the direction of the saloon.

"Yuh leavin' it at that?" asked Stryde as he drew closer. "Yuh lettin' them scum go?" His ice-blue eyes gleamed. "Well?"

"Yuh mean you're goin' after them?" said Raithe.

"In this weather?" followed Morgan. "F'Crissake, yuh'd never get — "

"Who's ridin'?" snapped Brent, glaring round the faces.

"Count me in," said Chester Woodley.

The others stayed silent.

"What about the doc?" said Morgan. "What's happened to him?"

"Reckon yuh'll find him safe enough," said Stryde. "Lori Baker with him." He paused, watching the faces. "But yuh'll find only the ashes of your barber."

"Doone's daughter couldn't have been fit to ride, could she?" murmured Brent to himself. "But in God's name, where they headin'?"

Heads turned again as Lou Fletcher's shop finally collapsed, its charred bones hissing and spluttering to their wet winter grave.

"Amen," sang the undertaker.

And all eyes turned, it seemed, to the pitch-black heavens that were suddenly weeping fresh snow.

14

CHESTER WOODLEY held his chin close to his chest, snuggled deeper into his winter coat, and reflected that maybe he was, after all, a mite too long in the tooth for this sort of thing.

Twenty years ago perhaps, but now the bones were getting brittle, the blood thinner, and stamina was in short supply, a bit like his breath. He shivered at another cruel whip of the wind. Even so, he pondered, no newspaperman worth a smudge of ink would miss a chance of trailing the Doones first-hand. That would be some story. Assuming he lived to tell it.

He lifted his eyes to glance quickly at the dark shape of Stryde up ahead. No arguing with that man, he reckoned. He would have ridden out of Remark alone if need be. When you had finally got to gunning one of the Doones and had the others in your sights, you kept going, whatever the odds. Stryde would keep going for just as long as it took.

He shivered again as Sheriff Brent's mount slithered through the snow to come alongside him. "Don't make no sense," grunted Brent against the whine of the wind. "Where's Doone headin' f'Crissake? There ain't nothin' out here 'til yuh hit the old stage post at Red Rocks, forty miles on. And if that gal of his is still bad . . . " The wind blew his words to the distant smears of breaking first light.

"Stryde'll have them figured," called Chester. "He won't let this chance slip away."

Brent reined his mount closer. "He got somethin' personal against the bunch?" he asked.

"Sure," said Chester, glad for a moment to forget the biting cold. "One of the critters killed the woman he was goin' to wed. She was travellin' on a stage from back east to join up with Stryde out at Carsway. Doones raided the stage, raped the woman, then shot her. Stryde was a marshal them days — good one at that — but he threw in his badge and vowed as how he'd spend the rest of his days trackin' the bunch down. I met him at Carsway, and we been close ever since." He glanced at Brent. "That was ten years back, and he ain't given up."

Brent stared at the rider ahead. "Don't look as if he's plannin' to neither."

"Not now he ain't. Not with one of the scum under his belt. Yuh can bet on that."

Chester Woodley lowered his chin again and snuggled into his coat.

Sheriff Brent fell silent and let his thoughts wander back to Remark — to Sam Baker, Ridge Parker, Charlie Grant, Lou Fletcher; to Sugar defying Malachy Doone, of flames licking the night sky, Stryde's ice-blue stare, the blaze of his Colt . . .

"Reckon the fella's right at that," he murmured.

* * *

Another hour of whipping wind, flurrying snow and biting cold had passed before Stryde raised an arm and called for Chester and Brent to rein into the lean cover of a bulge of rocks.

"Weather ain't easin' none," he said, gazing over the grey sweep of the bleak, empty land. "Doone's tracks are clear enough, but they're gonna fade if this snow keeps up." He ran a hand over the flakes clinging to his dark stubble. "They're movin' due south, but they're goin' to have to rest up soon. That gal ain't goin' to stay the pace. Any ideas where?"

"Ain't nothin' I know hereabouts, save the old stage post at Red Rocks," said Brent. "But, hell, that's miles on."

Chester grunted. "I heard tell as

how there used to be a fella out here who lived alone for years, a sorta recluse."

"Moses Fish," said Brent. "Sure, he had a place up in the hills. Never left it. Never once set foot in town. Went moon-swingin' mad, they say, and set fire to the whole outfit, includin' himself. That's all ages back."

"That fact or hearsay?" asked Stryde.

Brent shrugged. "Fact, I reckon — coloured up a mite."

Stryde turned his gaze to the emptiness. "Mebbe somethin' of the place is still standin'. Mebbe Doone'll find it."

"That's a long shot, mister," said Brent.

"It's all long shots right now," returned Stryde.

"Yuh reckon Doone'll figure on somebody trailin' him?" frowned Chester.

"He'll know," murmured Stryde. "He'll have smelled us by now." The icy stare tightened. "He hunts like an animal, and reacts the same when he's bein' hunted. But he's gotta real thorn in his paw right now — that daughter of his. She's gotta be slowin' them up. And Caleb ain't goin' to relish that fer long."

"But he sure as hell won't leave the money," said Chester.

Brent beat his arms across his chest. "Beats me why the critter pulled outa Remark so fast. He could've held out for days."

"But he couldn't stretch the odds," retorted Stryde. "Sooner or later he was goin' to be out-gunned. Doone don't wait for a hand like that t' be dealt. He scatters the pack."

The three men sat in silence for a while, their gazes sweeping the land, watching the morning light struggle for a hold from the funeral sky, the snow dancing on the wind.

"Goin' t' be a tough haul to them hills," said Chester.

"Will be if there's only the ghost

of Moses Fish when we get there," grunted Brent.

Stryde reined his mount clear of the cover and headed into the wind. He had his own hauntings to live with.

★ ★ ★

Caleb Doone waited until he had counted the three riders clear of the rocks before easing away from his own cover in the lower reaches of the hills.

Pa had been right, he thought, stumbling back through the snow to his mount, they were being followed, and at a pace. Should be some good hunting coming up, he grinned, specially if Celebration got to handling her guns again.

He frowned. She sure looked ill, and still bleeding at that. Might have been better if that stray shot at Lasserton had . . . He shuddered. Nothing had gone right since the day they had ridden into that sprawling town. Celebration hit, the darned weather, then Malachy going like he did. Never been a time like it before.

Everything had turned cold, and was somehow getting colder.

15

THEY worked hard at the trail for the next three hours. They struggled, cursed, slithered, slid and sweated, and sometimes, when the going got really tough for one of them, they would stop, catch their breath and lift their eyes to those darned hills — never that much closer, it seemed, and still shrouded in the grey mass of threatening snowfalls.

Sheriff Brent had another problem. Why, he wondered, were there no tracks of the Doones? How far ahead were they? Had they taken a different route? Or worse, had they skirted the hills altogether? Maybe all this effort would be a waste of time.

Chester Woodley had been too concentrated on keeping moving to let his thoughts wander. But he had figured that the mounts were getting close to exhaustion. If they kept going another hour, it would be a miracle. Same might be said for himself, he reckoned.

Stryde had only one target in mind: a sprawl of skinny brush and snarled tree stumps fronting a lift of boulders. If they could make it that far, they could rest up, take stock, and he and Brent could scout ahead on foot. Meantime, there was too much silence. The Doones were never that quiet for this long. And not when they were close.

Five minutes later he knew how close.

The shot boomed, whined and echoed high through the winter stillness, and was followed almost before it was silent by a second that seemed to rip the heavy clouds apart.

"Make for them rocks!" yelled Stryde as his mount bucked wildly.

A third shot scattered snow, but this was no shooting to kill or even maim, thought Brent. This was shooting to scare and scatter, and, darn it, it was doing just that!

"Keep movin', Chester," he shouted. "Can yuh handle that skitterin' mule?"

"Get to lookin' t' y'self, Jim Brent!" snapped Chester as his mount rolled threateningly.

More shots, some high, some low, but never wild; sharp as needles, probing and pushing the riders towards the brush and boulders.

Stryde was the first to reach them. "Sonofabitch!" he cursed, wiping snow from his eyes to peer at Brent and Chester Woodley as they rolled like lost logs. "He's got us where he wants us. Hell!"

"That Caleb somewheres up there?" asked Brent, squinting into the snowfall.

"That's Caleb," said Stryde. "But don't waste no lead on him. He's well hidden."

"What's he plannin'?" croaked Chester.

"He'll pin us down here for as long as he needs," said Stryde. "Then, when we're half stiff with cold, he'll pick us off one at a time." His eyes narrowed on the hillside. "Leastways, that's what he *thinks*."

★ ★ ★

Chester Woodley shivered, pulled half-heartedly at the collar of his coat and shuffled for a more comfortable position in his snow-bed. Hell, he was cold! Colder, he reckoned, than he could ever remember. Did you get this cold when you were dead?

He turned to look at Brent. The sheriff's gaze had not shifted from the hillside, as if he expected some part of it to move at any moment. Only time he seemed to blink was at the crack of a shot. But not even that seemed to bother Stryde. He simply sat with his back to a boulder and watched the snowfall. Thinking or waiting, wondered Chester, blowing into his hands? Both he reckoned.

"Critter keeps shiftin'," murmured

Brent. "He must be gettin' a mite tired by now."

Stryde grunted. "Thing is, he's still alone. Jubal and the girl ain't joined him."

"Could be they found that shack," said Chester.

Stryde shrugged and lifted his gaze to the darkening skies and the steady drift of snow. "Ten minutes, and I move," he announced flatly. "Cover me from here, but don't stir 'til I call yuh."

"And what if yuh don't?" said Brent.

"Figure it for y'selves."

★ ★ ★

Stryde went from the cover of the boulders like a dark, fleeting shadow of the winter's night; silent, fast, a foraging shape in silhouette.

He was bent low, his long coat dragging over the snow like mantling wings. He paused only occasionally to wait, watch, listen, then satisfied moved on again. Doone continued his sporadic firing, sometimes over the heads of Chester Woodley and Brent, sometimes to their left, their right, but never from the same vantage point.

Where would he move to next, wondered Stryde, and how much longer would he keep this up? He had to be waiting on an order from Jubal but where was he? Had he found the old shack? What sort of shape was his daughter in?

Stryde paused again, dismissed his thoughts, and wiped the icy dampness from his face. Hell, it was dark up here. He peered through the drifting snowfall. He reckoned he was still a deal short of where he figured Doone must be. But how to get closer without being spotted, or was Caleb already too preoccupied with his taunting to be expecting company?

Only one way to find out . . .

Stryde climbed on, silent as ever on the carpet of soft snow, but with a creeping doubt that one false step, a sudden fall on unseen ice, might be all that Doone would need to swing that Winchester round and blast the night apart.

"Hell!" he mouthed as he felt for his next hold on a steeper slope of the hill and dislodged a stone that tumbled away behind him, scattering the snow like white dust. He hesitated, half turned and then it was too late.

Stryde almost felt the Winchester before he saw its barrel snaking out of the darkness. The shape behind it was blurred and vague, wrapped in coats and scarves, but the eyes in the grim face were bright and mocking, as if Caleb Doone had been expecting Stryde to appear like an animal lured from its den to meet death.

Stryde had no time to reach for his Colt, and might have taken the full blaze of Doone's lead there and then had it not been for a sudden lift of the wind, a thicker, swirling flurry of snow that blinded both men for an instant but gave Stryde the chance to move.

He stepped to his right, lost his

footing on ice and fell back, his eyes wide on the blackness above him where Doone was sure to let the Winchester rip into life.

The shot came high as Doone shifted his stance and tripped. The rifle spun from his grip and he toppled in a blustering whirl of coats to crash at Stryde's side. There were seconds when neither man moved, when their eyes met like beams burning on a collision course, then Doone's fist crashed into Stryde's cheek, splitting the flesh.

"Sonofabitch!" gasped Doone, and struggled to his feet, at the same time lashing out with his boot at Stryde's thigh. Stryde took the blow, winced and reached through the flaps of his coat for his Colt. But Doone was already ahead of the move as his boot lashed out again, this time with deadly accuracy at Stryde's wrist to send the six-shooter spinning away to the darkness.

Now both men were on their feet, their arms cutting through the snowfall like swords, their feet fighting for precarious holds on the snow and ice.

Doone took a blow square to the jaw; Stryde's head shot back under the counter punch. Doone lunged, teeth bared, eyes flashing, but was sidestepped by Stryde. He lunged again and was within a fingertip hold of Stryde's shoulders when he skidded violently to his left and was aware too late of sliding down the hillside towards an outcrop of rocks.

Stryde watched him go as he might have watched an avalanche gather momentum; saw him bounce, jerk wildly, thud into the rocks; heard the cry of pain, the crack of bone, stared at the spread of blood over the snow — and waited in the wind until there was silence and Caleb Doone lay twisted and still, no more than a mound of clothes.

"Must've broken his neck," murmured Stryde as he turned back to the night. "Fittin' enough."

16

THE three men had waited in the deepest of the darkness for no more than minutes before reaching the same conclusion: Moses' old shack was deserted and had been for some time.

"But Doone's been there, sure enough," said Chester, squinting through the snowfall. "There's a drift of smoke. Must've lit a fire. Then what, f'Crissake? He just up and go? To where? Didn't wait for Caleb neither. Don't figure."

Sheriff Brent tipped the snow from the brim of his hat. "T'ain't goin' to do that gal no good draggin' her around like baggage. She ain't up to that in this weather."

Stryde put the flare of a match to a cheroot and blew a line of smoke. "Let's take a look," he said, his blue eyes dancing as he urged his mount forward.

Chester and Brent waited a moment before moving. "Malachy . . . now Caleb," murmured Brent, watching Stryde's back. "Don't he never get tired of killin'?"

"Not yet awhile," said Chester. "Not 'til he's had the three of them. And it's Jubal he wants more than any."

Brent sighed. "Yeah, well mebbe old man Doone's got other plans. He ain't goin' t' be no pushover."

"Same could be said fer Stryde there. Kinda keeps the odds even, don't it?"

Brent shrugged. Trouble with Chester Woodley, he reflected, as the three men edged towards the shack, he was writing next week's *Bugle* headline — the way he wanted it to happen! Brent reckoned the Doones had spent no more than a couple of hours in the shack. "Couldn't have been no longer," he said, once the three had lit a fire and could move about through the shadowy glow of it. "They had some sorta stab at a meal, made coffee, mebbe dried out their clothes. But after that . . . " He turned to Stryde. "What yuh reckon?"

Stryde stepped back to the light from a darker corner of the room where he had been examining a mound of worn blankets. "The Doone gal's gotten worse," he said. "She's bleedin' bad again. Fresh blood on them blankets, and plenty of it."

Chester Woodley lifted his hat and scratched the top of his head. "So why'd Jubal leave? Why risk the girl out there? What's he tryin' to do — kill her or somethin'?"

"Save her," said Stryde.

"*Save* her, f'Crissake! How'd yuh figure that?"

Stryde crossed to the fire and stood with his back to it. "*He's takin' her back to Remark.*"

There was a stunned, heavy silence broken only by the crackle of the fire. Chester glanced at Brent, then stared at Stryde. "Say that again," he croaked.

"That blood there's the answer," said

Stryde. "If the gal is bleedin' that bad Jubal'll know there ain't no point in tryin' to make it to Red Rocks, and he couldn't have stayed here. So he's only one choice: get the gal back to Doc at Remark — fast as he can."

"But if he does that . . . " began Brent.

"He'll have to give himself up," clipped Stryde. "That'll be the card he'll play — take me, but save the girl."

"Hell . . . " sighed Chester.

"And the haul from the raid?" asked Brent.

"That'll go with the deal." Stryde walked to the shadowed side of the fire. "Figure it," he went on. "Jubal's lost Malachy, and he's content enough to leave Caleb to his fate. His only concern is the girl. She always has been. Jubal won't be thinkin' no further than her, and if that means others dyin' and givin' himself up, so be it. He'll take his chances from there."

"Heck," said Brent, wiping a hand

across his suddenly damp brow, "if yuh right . . . "

"He's right," croaked Chester.

"If Doone's headin' back to Remark, I gotta shift. F'Crissake, I'm the sheriff there!"

"No hurry," said Stryde. "Doone's mebbe a good two hours ahead of us, but he ain't movin' fast. It's goin' to be all of first light before he hits town."

"So?" frowned Brent.

"So we collect Caleb's body — we're takin' him in — and see if we can round up his mount. Then we do the best we can for our own horses, dry out, get warm, and move when we're good and ready. We ain't settin' a foot on that trail 'til we reckon we can handle it."

"Makes sense," murmured Chester, gratefully.

"OK," said Brent, "so we do it your way. But I wanna know somethin' first." He paused and stared hard at Stryde. "Chester here's told me somethin' of yuh and what happened, and I sympathize. Doubtless would've done the same in your boots. But it seems to me that killin' the Doones is all yuh figure on. Mebbe that's right. Scum like them ain't a deal of right to livin'. Well, yuh sure as hell taken care of two of them, but what yuh goin' t' do about Jubal if he hands himself in? He'll stand trial, and he'll hang sure as night, but I don't figure a hangin' is quite the same in your book." Brent paused again. "Yuh'll be robbed of the chance of killin' him personal, won't yuh?"

Stryde stepped to the front of the fire, stared into the flames for a moment, then turned to face Brent, his blue eyes gleaming. "That's as mebbe," he drawled coldly.

"OK, OK," hustled Chester. "Let's get movin', shall we?"

★ ★ ★

The morning was grey and sullen on the touch of what passed for daybreak;

the air thin and freezing, the snowfall now no more than a flurry of loose flakes over the bleak, silent land.

The town of Remark huddled like black bodies waiting to be prodded into life, but there was neither life nor movement in that early spread of light on that morning. Only curls of dark smoke from stiff chimneys twisted on the wind. Remark, it seemed, slept on.

Reet Morgan was the first to spot the rider and his trailed mounts moving out of the hills. Shape of the man looked a deal familiar, he thought, rubbing at the windowpane of his room. Seen him before somewhere . . .

He waited until the rider had cleared the slopes and reached flatter snowscape before deciding he was not seeing things. He was watching Jubal Doone ride back into town!

Ten minutes later he had raised Isaiah Raithe, Doc Maloney and the undertaker and was standing with them at the far end of the empty street.

"What the hell's goin' on?" he mouthed, squinting against the sting of the cold at the still approaching rider.

"Yuh see what he's carryin'?" said Raithe. "White rag tied to his rifle. He's givin' up!"

"Jubal Doone surrenderin' . . . " murmured Morgan.

"But who's that slumped across the spare mount?" asked Doc. "Unless I'm very much mistaken . . . "

The undertaker shifted his feet in the snow, raised his eyes to the solemn grey light, and began to hum.

17

JUBAL DOONE sat his mount stiff and tight as if frozen into the saddle like some mournful winter ghost. His face was blotched from the cold and wind; snow and frost had hardened on his stubble, and his white hair was plastered deep into his neck. But his eyes were still piercingly dark, as watchful as a hawk's.

"This ain't no trickin'," he drawled, glancing at the white rag, then settling his stare like a shadow on the three men watching him. "M'gal here's a deal worse. She needs yuh help, Doc. So I'm givin' m'self up fer her sake." He spat violently into the snow. "That seems fair to yuh?"

"Yuh should never have left," said Doc. "It was too soon. I warned yuh."

"Yuh did at that, but that's all has-been. Yuh takin' m' terms?"

"Where are the others?" asked Raithe.

"Five miles back of me, I'd reckon." Doone's eyes darkened. "Savin' for Caleb. Don't figure he's made it."

"That the haul from the raid at Lasserton?" said Raithe, nodding towards the second trailed mount.

"Every last dollar."

"Never thought I'd see the day," croaked Morgan.

"Put yuh guns aside, Doone, and let's get outa this cold," snapped Doc. "That gal ain't goin' to get no healthier stuck here."

But Doc Maloney's eyes had already clouded with doubt and apprehension long before the trailed mount bearing the slumped body of Doone's daughter passed close to him. One look had been enough . . .

And so that strange, improbable party went in silence down the town's main street, a grey procession in the dead grey light.

★ ★ ★

News of Jubal Doone's arrival back in town and the circumstances of his surrender, spread faster than a warm plains' wind, and for a few hours at least the grip of winter seemed to ease as men gathered in the Boundless Saloon to chew over the story as it unfolded — with and without the facts.

Reactions were mixed: some reckoned as how it was pointless wasting sympathy on the girl: all that mattered was that Doone was snared and that, sure as hell, meant the end of the gang. Others reckoned Doone had shown another side of his character that set a man to wondering just how deep he really was. "He's done what any pa would do fer his gal, and that's somethin'."

Still others wanted nothing short of a hanging at noon. "Don't we owe that to Ridge, Charlie Grant, Lou and the Baker folk? And why not hang the murderin' bitch 'longside of Doone — save Doc the trouble of doctorin'!" One man wagered he would stroll down to Doc's place 'right now' and shoot Doone and the girl for the price of a bottle of whiskey, and then slumped into a drunken doze before anyone could lay the bet.

There was a flurry of activity at the news that Sheriff Brent, Chester Woodley and that 'gunslingin' stranger' were back in town — 'And trailin' Caleb Doone, stiff as a board'. And there was not a man in Remark an hour later who missed the sight of Jim Brent escorting Jubal Doone to the town jail. Even so, they watched in silence and did not go back to hanging talk until Brent and Doone had disappeared indoors.

"Should string 'em up t'night," demanded one. "Stark naked so's they feel the cold of death first."

It was at this point that Reet Morgan wondered if it was time to start watering down the liquor . . .

But it was closer to the settling of an early nightfall when Doc Maloney left his home with the most important news of the day.

★ ★ ★

The doc strode hurriedly through the slush and snow to the backroom of the saloon where, at a tap on the door, he raised Reet Morgan.

"Get across to the jail, fast," he ordered. "Tell Jim Brent t' leave the turnkey in charge, then join me at the *Bugle* office. Same goes for Raithe and the undertaker. No questions, Reet. Just do it!"

Fifteen minutes later, Sheriff Brent, Raithe, Morgan, Chester Woodley and the undertaker were gathered round the stove in the print-shop, their eyes fixed on Doc Maloney.

"Well?" asked Raithe, impatiently. "What now? What's happened?"

Reet Morgan lit a fresh cigar. Chester Woodley adjusted his cracked spectacles. The undertaker sniffed.

"It's the gal, ain't it?" said Brent.

"She's dead," murmured Doc with no more than a quick glance at the faces watching him. "A half-hour ago."

He paused a moment. "Wound had opened up again. She lost a lot of blood. Never stood a chance out there in the hills." He sighed. "She shouldn't have left. Shouldn't have let her."

"Nobody's blamin' yuh, Doc," said Brent. "Hell, yuh did more than she deserved. Don't f'get, she was one of the gang. She was a Doone, and lived up to the reputation."

"That's true," said Raithe. "She'd have hung anyhow."

"But that ain't the point," said Doc. "She was my patient, and she died. I ain't in the business of hurryin' folk to their death."

The undertaker sniffed.

"Won't be a deal of mournin' for her, that's for sure," said Morgan through a cloud of smoke. "Not the way this town's feelin' right now. More likely to start whoopin' it up."

"And yuh'd best keep an eye on that," snapped Brent. "I don't want no drunken brawlin' top of everythin' else."

Morgan examined the tip of his cigar.

"Well, now," grunted Chester, adjusting his spectacles again. "Question is, how's Jubal goin' to take the news?"

"Does he need to know?" quipped Morgan.

"Does it matter anyhow?" followed Raithe.

"*It matters*."

The voice came from the shadowed end of the shop. Heads swung round, eyes narrowed and probed the gloom, but no one spoke until Stryde had stepped to the edge of the light, his blue eyes bright on the faces turned to him.

"What yuh sayin'?" asked Brent.

"No more than yuh've already seen for y'selves," said Stryde. "Doone gave himself up for the sake of the gal. Man of his nature can't get to payin' a higher price."

"But there's damn all he can do about it now!" grinned Raithe. "He's here. We're holdin' him, and come an easin' of this weather he'll be shipped out to Lasserton for the biggest hangin' yuh've ever seen. That's the final price Doone is payin', mister, and make no mistake about it."

Morgan blew another cloud of satisfied smoke. "Always assumin' folk here don't get to callin' their own price."

"There'll be none of that sorta talk," growled Brent. "There'll be no lynchin' in my town."

Morgan shrugged. The undertaker closed his eyes. Raithe picked fluff from his coat.

"Even so," began Chester, "what Stryde here is really tryin' to say is — "

But that was as far as he got before the bustle and shouts from the street silenced him and tightened the faces of the others.

"Hey, Sheriff," came the call, "get y'self out here. Jail's goin' up in flames!"

Stryde's blue eyes darkened like the sudden fall of night.

18

"GODDAMMIT!" seethed Brent, stamping his feet in the snow and glaring at the smouldering remains of his office and jail. "Goddammit, how the hell did he do it? Just how, f'Crissake?"

Reet Morgan plunged his hands into his pockets and hunched his shoulders against the freshening snow-licked wind. "Who's next? Lou's place, now this . . . Hell, Jim, at this rate Doone'll burn the whole town down! And where is he now?"

Isaiah Raithe sighed. "The cost'll be enormous. How the hell we're goin' to raise — "

"To hell with the costs!" fumed Brent. "I ain't interested. I wanna know how . . . "

"Doone had a knife on him," said Doc Maloney, quietly. "Well hidden,

I'd guess. I seen the body of the turnkey. He was stabbed clear enough. Doone must've sweet-talked the fella close. Don't take a lot of figurin'."

"Goddammit!" fumed Brent again.

"So like I say," said Morgan, producing a cigar and lighting it, "where's Doone now? We gotta get to him, and fast. Otherwise, this town'll be just a heap of dead bodies and ashes."

The undertaker raised his eyes to the night-black heavens and began to hum.

"Well, he ain't left town, I'll wager that," said Chester Woodley.

"So?" said Morgan, spreading his arms.

"So we start lookin'," said Raithe. "Hunt the critter down like the vermin he is."

"*That's just what yuh don't do.*"

Stryde stepped from the shadows and stood tall, taut, feet apart in the snow, his eyes brightening in the glow of the dying fire.

"Yuh got a better notion, mister?" asked Raithe.

"If it means more killin' and burnin' . . ." croaked Morgan.

"Give the fella a chance," snapped Brent, then, turning to Stryde, "Say your piece, mister."

Stryde waited a moment, relaxing, his fingers idling over the butt of his Colt. "Doone's here, and he ain't goin' no place," he began. "There ain't no point in him ridin' out. There ain't nowhere to go not yet, not 'til he can take the girl."

"But she's dead," said Morgan.

"Doone don't know that, does he? Nobody told him. He's figurin' on her mebbe bein' fit enough to leave in, say, a day. Meantime, he needs to get his hands on as much of that money as he can carry. He needs horses, blankets, food. But most of all, he needs to leave as much chaos behind him as he can raise to give him a clear run outa town. That's what he's plannin'."

Stryde paused, his gaze steady and

fixed on the faces watching him. "He'll hole-up wherever he can, changin' wherever it suits. He'll kill when it's necessary, burn when the fancy takes him. If yuh go scuttlin' about after him, he'll pick you off like flies. So yuh don't."

"And do what?" asked Raithe.

"Sheriff here clears the town before tempers and liquor take a hold. Get everybody indoors. Then yuh take over the saloon, hold it, watch and wait. And strike when you're sure."

"Yuh sayin' we give Doone the run of the town?" clipped Morgan.

Stryde nodded. "If yuh don't, undertaker here'll have a heart attack."

The undertaker's humming ceased, his eyes widened. "Lord save my soul for His good works," he murmured.

"OK," growled Brent, rubbing his chin thoughtfully. "We give it a try. Mebbe we'll get lucky."

★ ★ ★

It took Sheriff Brent, Isaiah Raithe and Reet Morgan close on two hours to clear the saloon and street of Remark's anxious and excited population and ensure that they were firmly indoors, some to watch with mounting curiosity from darkened windows, others to drift into drunken sleep.

"And let's just hope they stay put," said Raithe when he and the others, along with a barman and three of Morgan's sidehands, were finally gathered in the now dimly lit saloon.

"Won't see dawn if they don't," mused Chester Woodley, cleaning his spectacles.

"And now what?" asked Morgan, impatiently. "We just goin' to sit here, watchin' each other? Me, I got other things round here to attend to." He shrugged when Sugar, who had been tending Lori Baker in an upstairs room, gave him a cold, dismissive glare and wandered to the far end of the bar. "Well, mebbe they can wait awhile," he added gloomily.

"Seems to me," announced Raithe, gripping the lapels of his coat importantly, "we're takin' a helluva gamble with all this. Supposin' Doone does somethin' we ain't anticipatin'. What then? He could keep us on a knife-edge for hours, even days. Wouldn't it be a deal more sensible if we — "

"No!" snapped Brent, and was instantly silent again.

"It's the girl," said Doc, quietly. "She's the key. Doone won't rest 'til he's got to her, but he's gotta be sure it's safe enough."

"And when he does . . . " grinned Morgan. "When he sees her lyin' there in your place dead as — "

"Wouldn't dwell on that," quipped Chester.

The undertaker cleared his throat carefully and began to hum.

"Hold it!" hissed Brent from the saloon window. "Don't move, none of yuh."

"What's goin' on?" asked Raithe.

"Somebody out there. 'Cross at your store."

"The store, f'Crissake!" Raithe sprang to the batwings like an animal pouncing to its prey.

"No!" yelled Brent.

The roar and blaze of rifle fire shattered the night silence, ripped into the saloon splintering woodwork, sending showers of glass to the air, across the floor. Bodies dived, scrambled, slithered for cover through the dying light.

Brent fell back against the wall, his eyes wide in an unblinking stare on Raithe's hat as it skimmed into the darkness and its owner followed in a wild flight of limbs.

19

STRYDE eased deeper into the darkness of the deserted forge at the livery, closed his eyes and listened to the rage of rifle fire.

It would take Doone just four minutes to be certain he had those inside the saloon pinned down and too scared to raise an eyebrow, let alone a head, then he would scoop up his loot from the store and make for his next target: horses.

Stryde swallowed on a dry throat. Things were getting tighter, closer, like a knot sliding to its final grip. And this time it *would* grip, he thought, conscious of the cold sweat across his shoulders. This time there would be no mistakes, no near misses. Jubal Doone was going to end his murderous days right here in Remark, in the hell of the snow and freezing cold, in sight of the stare of the man who . . .

The firing ceased; night slipped back to its silent emptiness. Stryde opened his eyes and peered through the gloom to the dim shafts of light in the street. Doone would have to cross through them, and he would be in a hurry. Time was running out if he was going to clear the town before daybreak.

Stryde swallowed again, tapped the butt of his Colt, shifted his feet and watched the street as if expecting it to move. It was another minute before he saw the shadow that was out of place; taller, thinner, edging through the darkness, pausing, waiting its chance.

Doone made his dash when he was facing the livery. He went low but sure-footed over the snow, clutching his haul from the store close to him, and passed into the stabling without stopping.

Stryde heard his steps beyond the forge, the heavy breathing, the silence as he rested, thinking, scheming his next move, but relaxed in the satisfaction that he had come this far without a hand, or gun, raised against him.

Stryde could almost see the man's soft smile . . .

★ ★ ★

Sheriff Brent blinked the smoke and sting of cordite from his eyes, struggled to his feet, and peered into the gloom of the shattered saloon.

"Somebody get some lights, f'Crissake!" he bellowed, and listened to the clatter as the barman went in search of a lantern. "Doc?" he called again. "Doc — yuh OK?"

"OK," answered Maloney. "I got Raithe here. He's been hit."

"Chester, where are yuh?"

"Right here, Jim. Lost my specs fer a minute. Got 'em."

"One of m' men's shot right through," shouted Morgan.

"Where the hell are them lights?" snapped Brent.

The glow from the flickering lanterns revealed a bar room that looked as if it had been the setting for some desperate town war, with a whirlwind thrown in for good measure.

"Hell," croaked Chester Woodley. "When Doone gets mad, he sure goes plumb crazy!"

Brent crossed to where Doc Maloney was tending Raithe. "How bad?" he asked.

"Shoulder wound. Bad enough, but he'll live," said Doc.

Brent grunted and gazed round him. "OK, let's get this place cleaned up. And get some more lights, dammit!" He frowned. "Anybody seen Sugar?"

"Guess she'll be lookin' to Mrs Baker," said Morgan.

Brent grunted again, walked to the batwings and studied the empty street. The store opposite was quiet now, deserted, its broken windows staring like a corpse's open eyes on the darkness. Doone had moved on. The livery, wondered Brent, or Doc's place?

He sighed heavily. Wherever, time had come to put an end to all this. Leaving Doone loose in the town was as good as inviting him to destroy it. No telling where he might hit next.

"Know what yuh thinkin', Jim," said Chester Woodley at his side. "But you're wrong."

Brent looked at him. "Oh, and how'd yuh figure that? If this goes on, there'll be nothin' left, save the dead bodies. And what's Doone goin' to do when he finds out his daughter's dead? That'll be enough to crack him wide open. I can't take that risk, Chester. I'm wearin' the badge."

Chester examined his spectacles. "Sure," he said, quietly. "And you're packin' as fast a gun as this town's seen in a sheriff. No disputin' that. You're a fine lawman, Jim, and Remark's got good reason to be grateful to yuh, but there's a man out there who's given a slice of his life to get this close t' the Doones. I reckon yuh owe him the chance to finish it — his way."

Brent ran a hand over the shape of the batwings. "Easy to say, but Stryde's flesh and bone like the rest of us."

"Same goes for y'self, Jim. But there's a difference. Stryde's hate is black as Hell. Yours ain't no more than a deepenin' shade of grey. That gives Stryde the edge in my reckonin'. All you got to do is give him the time."

They fell silent and watched the snowfall drift through the night.

★ ★ ★

Stryde tensed at the scuff of Doone's boots through straw, then flexed his fingers, relaxed his breathing, and listened.

Doone was certain he was alone. He sensed nothing of another presence. Fine, thought Stryde, just fine. Maybe he had an edge over the old fellow. Maybe now was the time to use it.

He crept softly to the gap in the partition that led through to the stabling, drew his Colt as he reached it, and waited. He could still hear the rasp of Doone's breathing, smell the lingering closeness of smoke that clung to his clothing, imagine the fiery glare in the man's eyes as his thoughts raced. This was the moment . . .

Stryde swung himself through the gap, the Colt firm in his hand and aimed clear on the shadowy bulk facing him. He was aware in a split-second of the flash of Doone's eyes, the hiss of breath like a rattler disturbed, and then of nothing save the searing pain in his arm as the barrel of Doone's Winchester crashed across it.

Stryde winced, felt his fingers go limp, heard the Colt thud to the floor. He groaned, but moved instinctively ahead in a thrusting lunge into Doone's chest. Doone fell back with a spitting curse, raised the rifle and brought it down like a bolt of lightning on what should have been Stryde's head — but Stryde had already spun to his left, thudded into the partition and rolled forward.

His Colt . . . where the hell was the Colt?

"Sonofabitch!" spat Doone as his grip tightened on the rifle. "Sonofa . . ." The Winchester sliced through the air again, missing Stryde's right shoulder by a hair's-breath. Doone roared like a caged wild animal as Stryde lunged again, this time with his arms outstretched, fingers clawing for a hold on the bulk in front of him.

Stryde stretched, reached, smelled the stench of Doone's stale breath, caught the flash of the man's eyes, the scowl creasing his face, but felt nothing, held nothing as he dived on, crashing head-first into the far wall of the stabling.

He was aware for a moment of blinding lights, a spinning swirl of stars, a descending silence that drowned him, and then of darkness, empty of all sounds and movements.

Jubal Doone stood over the body then prodded the rifle barrel into the man's ribs. Lifeless, clean out. "Darn fool," he murmured. "But I ain't goin' to shoot yuh, mister, whoever yuh are. No, I reckon I'll have me another blaze . . ." He grinned. "Yeah, burn the whole flea-crawlin' town to nothin'."

Ten minutes later Doone had cleared the livery of the few remaining mounts, taken a lantern from the forge, lit it and tossed it into the deepest spread of straw.

Then he left, a laughing, darting shadow, as the flames leapt high behind him.

20

SUGAR slid through the shadows at the rear of the undertaker's and waited in the side alley facing the deserted street. She was cold, almost too cold to move let alone think. She shivered and tried to snuggle deeper into her clothes.

Hell, she must be half-crazed, she thought, squinting through the flurries of fresh snow. How in tarnation had she ever got to figuring she could help a man like Stryde? If he was out there — and he had to be somewhere — he was more than capable of handling trouble as he found it.

Even so, she knew Jubal Doone; knew him better than most, the way he thought, schemed, and went ahead with whatever ruthless planning crossed his mind. The weeks of being forced to ride with the gang had taught her a good deal about the Doones. And now there was only Jubal of the rotten bunch left.

She shivered again. He was more than enough.

She stepped back at the sudden snort of a horse. A rider? Doone? No, a mount thundering loose, followed by another. Four of them. The livery! Hell, Jubal must have fired it!

It was then that she saw the glow, the lick of flames, and began running towards them.

★ ★ ★

Stryde had not moved, not even as the heat of the flames deepened and the smoke thickened. But now he stirred at the sound of a distant voice that seemed urgent, beckoning, as if willing him to move closer to it. Then he felt the tug at his shoulder, hands that gripped but had no strength to lift. The voice, the hands . . .

But it was the violent rush of cold

over his head, into his face and down his neck that made him shudder into life and open his eyes.

"Sorry," said Sugar, kneeling at his side. "Couldn't figure no other way of bringin' yuh round." She tossed aside another handful of snow. "Best move, mister," she added, struggling to her feet. "We got just minutes before this lot comes down on top of us."

They stumbled from the livery like blown splinters of the flaming timbers, their feet slithering through snow and slush, bodies bent against the showers of dancing sparks. Stryde dragged Sugar into the deepest shadows and held her close as they turned to watch the livery roof collapse in a crunching, hissing mass of flames.

"Doone do that?" asked Sugar.

Stryde grunted. "I owe yuh for what yuh did back there, ma'am. Ain't many women would've — "

Sugar eased away from his hold. "Just lucky I happened by," she smiled. "Here." She delved into the depths of her coat and handed Stryde his Colt. "Kinda stepped on this. Figured yuh might be needin' it." Her eyes shone in the glow of the still burning livery.

Stryde grunted again, but stiffened at the bellow of voices and rush of bodies at the far end of the street. "Town's on the move," he murmured. "Give 'em my apologies. I got other business."

And then he was lost in the night.

★ ★ ★

Stryde hugged the thicker shadows at the rear of the town buildings and went as fast as the deeper snow would permit in the direction of Doc Maloney's place.

His head still throbbed and his line of vision danced through blurs and smudges. He had taken one hell of a beating back there in the livery, but Doone had failed to finish the job. He halted, wiping his eyes. He was alive — thanks to Sugar and the edge was still there, just as long as he could see it. And find Doone.

He waited, listening to the babble of voices at the livery, imagining the confusion, the mounting anger. It would take only a handful of hotheads to set the townsfolk in a lynching mood. And they would have no doubts where to head once the news of Doone's daughter's death was out. But maybe there was still time, he reflected, blinking for a steady focus. Maybe Doone would be too shocked, too bewildered to move once he was certain the girl was dead.

He turned his coat collar high into his neck and thrust himself back to the now driving snowfall.

It took Stryde another ten minutes to come to the rear of Doc's home. There was a clear line of footprints through the snow to the back door. Doone was in there, sure enough, but there were no lights, no sounds, no movements. Had he left?

Stryde shrugged against the cold, the

biting wind. This was no place to be hanging about. He had to get closer; better still inside. He listened to the muffled babble of voices, the occasional shout. How long before the mob were fired up? How long before Sheriff Brent lost control?

Stryde stepped to the back wall of the building, pressed himself to it; waited, listened. No sounds. He blinked, steadied his vision. There was a window far side of the door. Maybe he would be able to see inside, or dare he risk opening the door? Was it locked?

Stryde swallowed and moved again.

There was nothing to be seen through the window, but the door eased open softly when Stryde turned the knob. He watched the inch space like a hawk. The wind scuttled to the gap, moved the door another inch, but the silence beyond it stayed tight.

Stryde drew his Colt, pushed the door open, winced at the squeak, and prayed that the sound would be lost on the wind.

* * *

A room to the right, another ahead at the end of a narrow hallway. Stryde took a single step, halted, began to sweat. His head ached, his eyes watered. The Colt was suddenly heavy in his hand.

Another step . . .

And then he was able to see the shadowy shapes in the room.

Doone stood with his head bent in an unmoving stare at the body on the table before him. The girl had been covered to her neck with a sheet, but her golden hair and white waxen face were clear in the pool of pale winter light.

"Didn't reckon on things pannin' out like this, gal," murmured Doone to the body. "Not one bit. Nossir. Your brothers, Malachy and Caleb, gone . . . darn fools. Never had a snick of smartness through their heads. Not never. And now, y'self." He sighed deeply. "Never should've reckoned we were keen enough for Lasserton. Job too big — and we were fallin' apart, sure enough, just like yuh warned me. Oh, yes, yuh warned me. Can hear yuh now. Yuh said, didn't yuh, that we shouldn't hit Lasserton. Don't hit Lasserton, Pa, yuh said. Can hear yuh sayin' so now. Yuh knew, gal, yuh knew ... Should've listened to yuh for once, 'stead of bein' plain mule-stubborn." He sniffed. "Well, there yuh are. Got nobody t' blame but m'self. Nobody. Always figured I knew best. Gettin' old, gal, gettin' real old ... "

He paused. His left hand moved to touch the cheek of the cold, dead face, the fingers shaking, hovering. "Sure am goin' t' miss yuh, Celebration. No mistakin'. Miss yuh like hell I am. Yuh always were the closest." The fingers settled, touched, then came away sharply as if shocked at what they had discovered. "Be seein' yuh, gal. Be seein' yuh, real soon . . . "

Stryde licked the sweat from his top lip, took a firmer grip on the Colt, and shifted his feet.

"Easy, Jubal, real easy. Hands where I can see 'em," he croaked through the gloom.

Doone swung round with all the vicious intent of a disturbed rattler, his Winchester levelled at his hip. A smile broke and twisted at his lips; his eyes brightened and did not blink in the sudden, shattering roar of the rifle that seemed to rock the house to its foundations.

When Stryde had struggled back to his feet and wiped his eyes clear of smoke, there was no one there.

21

STRYDE plunged into the room, his eyes in a frenzy of probing for Doone's escape route. A door ahead, open ... leading where? He halted, waited, listened. His free hand brushed against the sheeting covering the body, and for a moment he shivered as his gaze turned and settled on the face of Celebration Doone.

She looked serene and peaceful now, a once beautiful young woman who would have tantalized any man with the sparkling lure of her smile — and then shot him while he drooled.

"Bitch!" he muttered, and plunged on to the open door.

Seconds later, Stryde stood alone in the empty street, the snowfall dancing at his head and shoulders, the cold seeping into him. The townsfolk were still occupied with dousing the livery fire; the saloon stood dark and silent; slow smoke swung to the wind from the charred shell of the sheriff's office. The rest of Remark lay in the grip of a winter's night, shadow-filled and bleak as ice.

But somewhere in the emptiness and silence, Jubal Doone waited and watched, that Winchester barrel snaking eerily over the darkness.

Stryde stiffened, wiped his eyes, flexed his hold on his Colt. With any luck, Brent and the others had been too confused and intent on the fire to be drawn by the sound of the shots at Doc Maloney's. Maybe they would stay that way. But Doone what in hell's name was he planning next?

Finding a mount might not be so difficult, but where would he ride to? What hope was there in a frozen land without warmth and food? No, that would not be Doone's style. He would not run — not now, decided Stryde. He would shoot it out, and bury half of Remark in the madness.

"If the sonofabitch has the chance," he murmured, and slid away to the next deep shadow.

Stryde moved slowly, watchfully, certain that Doone had already occupied the ground he wanted to hold to the bitter end, however fate and his wily instincts dealt the hand.

He paused where the darkness was deepest; seconds in which to peer ahead through his still clearing vision, tip the snow from his hat, take a new grip on the Colt, and shrug against the tension stiffening his limbs.

Hell, he was cold!

Another few yards, another shadow.

He turned quickly to glance at the glow of the livery fire burnished bright copper on the thick night sky, the empty slush and snowswept street, to listen to the sounds of men echoing on the wind.

How long would it be before . . . ?

And then he heard the sound.

The creak and muffled thud of a door closing; footsteps on the boardwalk ahead. Silence again, save for the whine of the wind. More footsteps, closer now and closing. Purposeful steps, unafraid. A darker, thicker shape began to grow in front of him. It had eyes, icy and staring, a voice that seemed to move across the darkness as if propelled by some lost shadow-ghost.

"You're gettin' on m' nerves, mister, whoever yuh are," said Doone in slow, deep, measured tones.

His face, clearer now in the limp light, was taut and hollowed, the lips no more than a ragged scrawl over the flesh, the eyes narrowing under the grey hoods of lids. The wind lifted the strands of his straggling hair.

"Who are yuh, anyhow, in God's name?"

Doone levelled the Winchester from his hip and spat at a flurry of snow that swirled at his cheeks and chin.

Stryde stayed silent, unmoving, his gaze like a fixed light on Doone's face.

"Talkative, ain't yuh?" croaked

Doone. "Don't matter none. There ain't the time fer pleasantries and passin' talk." He spat again. "S'pose you're responsible fer the killin' of m'boys, eh? You did that? That your doin', mister? I'm reckonin' so." The man's eyes narrowed. "Well, now, that's a mighty high price yuh goin' t' pay for the privilege. Mighty high. High as it comes — with yuh Goddamn life! Yuh hearin' that, mister? Yuh got it clear in yuh head? I said *with yuh life.*"

The butt of Stryde's Colt was suddenly damp in his hand; a trickle of sweat slid from beneath his hat, but he felt nothing of the bite of the cold, saw nothing save the shape of Doone, the glint in his eyes, the stiff, steady, unrelenting aim of the rifle.

"Carsway," he murmured. "Remember Carsway, Doone? Yuh held up the stage close by. Yuh killed m'woman." Stryde's words creaked on the freezing air. "We were plannin' to wed."

A faint grin flickered at Doone's

lips. "That so? Kinda nice, eh? A fella should wed. Keeps him sobered up, God fearin'. Good woman's like a new blanket, mister: wraps yuh warm against the sonofabitch evils of this Goddamn life. Ain't that so? Shame yuh missed out." The grin flickered again like a wet smear on darkness. "Yuh never got to knowin' nothin' of bein' wed, did yuh? Shame. Yuh should've gotten y'self another woman. Would've saved all this, wouldn't it? Kept yuh breathin'."

Stryde's reaction through his exploding hatred was to shift one foot — a step that wiped the grin from Doone's lips as he eased back, hunched his shoulders and let the Winchester roar into life.

Even as Stryde ducked away to his left he felt the burning rip of the shot missing his cheek by no more than the lift of his stubble.

He slithered into the snow, gripped the Colt, but had already lost sight of Doone when the second shot blazed over his body.

"Sonofa-hellfire-bitch!" yelled Doone. "Yuh killed m'boys, damn yuh! Yuh killed 'em . . ."

Stryde rolled into the ice-cold slush, shuddered, gasped, struggled to come to his knees, and waited for another roar and rip of lead that would surely blast his head to pulp.

He had rolled again, soaked now to the skin, when a sudden rush of light from swinging lanterns sprayed the street behind him with an amber glow. Voices clamoured on the air; feet sloshed and splashed through snow and slush. Stryde scrambled again and rose, sodden and dripping, to face the headlong surge of men slithering towards him from the livery.

"Back! F'Crissake get back!" he shouted.

But the throng came on, lanterns swaying, shadows leaping and lunging over the snow, voices crowded in a pitch of shouts and yells.

"No!" croaked Stryde, his own voice lost in the numbed agony of the freezing cold that gripped him. "No, damn yuh, back! Get back!"

He swung round again. Doone . . . where was Doone?

The Winchester roared with shots that went high and wild as if aimed at the snowflakes in the wind-swirled flurry.

And then there was silence.

The amber glow shimmered. The shadows lay still. The voices died.

"I'll rip the lot of yuh t' gut-soaked flesh!" screamed Doone, and swung the rifle through a blazing arc of spitting lead. "All of yuh, every last one of yuh. Yuh hear that? Yuh hearin' me?"

Stryde was already moving, plunging into the darkness beyond the glow; bent double, soaked, his vision blurred, his head throbbing, and the sweat of the effort oozing to the ice-tight cold in his limbs.

But the Colt lay firm in his hand and the aim was steady when his finger squeezed and vengeance spat from the very marrow of his bones.

Doone's rifle roared again, the shots ripping into the night like lightning. "Go t' the Devil, damn yuh!" he yelled as Stryde came on, slithering to the left, stumbling to the right, his legs working instinctively through his surge of hatred.

"You're goin' to die, Doone," cursed Stryde. "You're goin' t' die right here, in this town, in this street." He slithered on. "You're goin' t' go down cold as the snow at your Goddamn feet!"

Stryde felt the heat of the Colt pulse through his fingers, the shudder of it as it spat. He slid into deeper slush and blinked, almost blinded by the splash of the filth, then stood his ground, gritted his teeth, and watched his last shots rip with remorseless accuracy into Doone's chest.

Doone stumbled at the first blaze of pain, fell back choking on a mouthful of blood. The Winchester roared its final defiance to an empty sky.

His arms hung lifeless for a moment at his sides, his eyes widened, mouth opened, closed, dribbled blood. He retched, then lifted his arms high above his head and called into the night:

"Yuh just hang on there, Celebration . . . Yuh hear me, gal? Yuh just wait f' your old Pa. I'm a-comin', gal. Yuh pa's comin', goin' t' be right there at your side . . . Just like we always been, gal, just like we always were . . . wait, gal, wait . . . "

Jubal Doone's eyes widened again, round and staring as if seeing deeper into the bowels of oblivion. Then he turned and dragged his bent body through shuffling, scuffing steps along the street towards the darkness of the bleak winter-land at the end of it.

Ten, eleven, twelve steps . . .

The Winchester slid from his grip. The wind caught at the strands of his long white hair. He halted, turned his head to look back at the brooding shadows of the town of Remark, and fell face-down through the flurrying snow to where it lay in death-cold welcome.

"Go t' Hell, Jubal Doone," murmured Stryde. "Go to the Hell of your makin'."

22

CHESTER WOODLEY adjusted his eye-shade and peered over his dusty spectacles at the trays of typefaces on the bench in front of him.

His fingers slid affectionately, thoughtfully over the array of fonts. Well, it sure was going to be a difficult choice, he pondered, beginning to hum quietly to himself. There had never been a time in Remark such as this since ... "Since never, I guess," he murmured.

How to tell it, just as it happened, that was the problem. No frills, no make-believe dramatics; nothing save the facts as they stood — with maybe just a mite of colour for atmosphere. Well, maybe ... maybe not.

Hell, he thought, when you came square on to it the town had made history, been right there at the centre of it; sort of standing witness to it. Why, folk would be recounting the events for years, decades, maybe forever. Living through the legend that would grow. A story handed down, generation to generation, for all time.

"Yeah, and gettin' fancier with the tellin'," he muttered.

Well, there would be none of that, not of his doing, that was for sure. It would be the facts; hard, real, as they were. The true story of how the reign of the Doones was finally ended.

Nothing hurried. No way; it would be considered . . .

Chester rubbed his chin, turned from the bench and crossed to the window of the *Bugle* print-shop. One hell of a day out there, he mused. Clear blue sky, warm wind cruising soft as a breath from the south-west, snow melting, town coming back to life, the dark days and nights behind them. Some day . . .

A day the Doones would never see.

Theirs were over.

"Last days of the Doones," he murmured. "Yeah, that's the truth of it right enough. Just as it happened."

He smiled softly, wiped his hands on his apron, flexed his old fingers enthusiastically, and went back to the bench.

Just as it happened.

★ ★ ★

Sheriff Jim Brent stood in the warm sunlight bathing the boardwalk and watched Isaiah Raithe cross the street towards him.

Raithe was a worried man, and it showed, thought Brent, noting the slump to the man's shoulder where Doone's shot had hit him, the fidgety steps, the darker than usual shadows at his eyes. Sleepless nights, that was his trouble, and maybe with good reason: Sam Baker dead and his widow a suffering soul; Charles Grant, dead; Lou Fletcher, dead, and the livery no more than ashes; Brent's own office a charred shell; the store smashed . . .

Gentlemen of the town committee would have some weighty matters to discuss when they got to it. Hell, would they!

"How's the shoulder?" asked Brent as Raithe stepped alongside of him.

"Painful, Jim, painful, 'specially at night, but t'ain't nothin' against all this." He swept an arm loosely over the street. "Darn near half the town burned out, m' store wrecked, saloon the same, men dead . . . I tell yuh straight, Jim Brent, t'ain't goin' to be no party puttin' this lot t' rights. Nossir. And the cost . . . the cost. Hell, m'figurin' is goin' clear outa reality. Hundreds, hundreds. And maybe thousands. Yuh realize that? Thousands."

"But we got the Doones, and the money they took," said Brent.

"So we did. So we did. Leastways, that fella Stryde did." Raithe ran a hand over his face. "And speakin' of him, where the devil is he? Ain't seen hide nor hair of him fer days. He gone t' ground or somethin'?"

"Restin' up," said Brent. "Earned it too."

Raithe grunted. "Yeah, and that's another thing. What we goin' t' do about him? Yuh figured that? He stayin' on here, ridin' out, or what?"

"Don't reckon anybody gets t' doin' anythin' about a fella like Stryde," said Brent. "He'll do just as he pleases, and no interferin'. Way I see it, I'll wager he'll be on the first train outa here."

"Well," reflected Raithe, "suit himself, I guess. Can't say fairer. We ain't got no call on him, that's fer sure, savin' to thank him."

"Wouldn't make too much of that, either. Stryde had his own good reasons for levellin' with the Doones. Kinda personal. Take my advice, yuh'll leave it at that. Best way."

Raithe grunted again. "Mebbe so. Could be, o'course, that the gentlemen of the town committee have other ideas. T'ain't in our nature t' be turnin' our backs on good deeds, in spite of the formidable work facin' us." He sniffed. "Must make sure we put a vote of thanks on the next agenda. Only fittin'. And mebbe some sorta presentation. Nothin' too elaborate — or expensive — o'course. Just a token. Yeah, a token. Yuh think so, Jim?"

Brent blinked and slid his hands to his pockets. "I'm sure the gentlemen will make the right decision."

"Naturally," said Raithe. "S'what we here for. Meantime, I hear as how Sam Baker's brother's ridin' in from Big Bend to look to Lori. Doc figures she'll be OK in a week or so. That's somethin'." He sighed and flicked at a speck of mud on his coat. "Sure has been one helluva time. Sets yuh to wonderin' how we pulled through."

"Here's one who ain't complainin'," said Brent, nodding to the approaching figure of the undertaker. "Mornin', Adam," he called. "Yuh still keepin' busy?"

The undertaker raised his hat and

smiled. "The Lord's work is never done, gentlemen. Never done . . ."

★ ★ ★

It was mid-afternoon two days later when the first train bound for Big Bend pulled into Remark.

Gathered at the rail office to meet it were Sheriff Brent, Chester Woodley, Isaiah Raithe, Doc Maloney, Reet Morgan, and the undertaker. The single passenger set to board the train that day was the man the town had only ever known as Stryde.

"Well, now," began Isaiah Raithe, clutching the lapels of his coat, "I guess this is where yuh take leave of us, mister. Sorry t' see yuh go. Real sorry." He cleared his throat and glanced quickly round the gathering. "Yes . . . real sorry. But, as we all know, times moves on and what has been will be. Yes . . ."

"Amen," murmured the undertaker. Reet Morgan blew a cloud of smoke from his cigar. "Time ain't never done a deal more, I'd say," he smiled.

Raithe raised his voice. "And we all been through a tryin' time. Real tryin'."

"Amen," murmured the undertaker again.

"T'ain't been easy," continued Raithe. "But the gentlemen of the town committee are real grateful to yuh, Mister Stryde. Can't say fairer."

"That's a fact," said Chester.

"And amen again," said the undertaker, lifting his eyes.

"Too many amens, Adam," drawled Morgan. "This ain't no burial."

"True enough," said Raithe, "but a sad occasion for all that. We would just like t' say . . ."

Sheriff Brent coughed loudly. "Yuh just take care now, fella. And don't go overlookin' us next time yuh happen this way."

"Sure thing," murmured Chester.

"Welcome at my place any time," grinned Morgan. "We'll have it lookin' a deal tidier next time you're in town."

Stryde nodded. "I'll hold yuh to it."

"Meantime," began Raithe again, then turned with the others as a buckboard clattered to a halt at the backside.

"Well, I'll be darned," mouthed Morgan, dropping his cigar. "Now what in tarnation is she doin' here?"

"Afternoon, gentlemen," said Sugar, stepping to the ground. "This train bound for Big Bend?"

"Yuh mean you're leavin'?" gaped Raithe.

"'Bout the size of it, Mister Raithe," smiled Sugar, moving to collect her valise.

"Now hold hard there," snapped Morgan. "This some sorta joke or somethin'? What kinda nonsense you talkin', Sugar?"

"No nonsense, Reet," said Sugar. "And no joke."

"But yuh can't just up and out like that. T'ain't the done thing. Yuh can't. Darn it, woman, I ain't lettin' yuh!"

"That so?" Sugar adjusted her bonnet.

"Well, yuh can just get t' thinkin' again, 'cus I sure as hell am leavin' on this train."

"And where d'yuh reckon you're goin'?" said Morgan. "Who's goin' to look to yuh? Let me tell yuh somethin' — yuh ain't got a hope out there." He fumbled for another cigar. "I look after yuh, and that's final."

"No, Reet, that's just what yuh don't do." Sugar swirled her skirts. "Not no more yuh don't. I'm headin' for a fresh start. Get the smell and feel of them Doones right outa m' skin. Forever. Yuh got your town, and yuh got more than enough t' occupy yuh here without distractions from me. Yuh follow?"

"Oh, my," murmured the undertaker.

"Lady's got her own choices," said Doc Maloney.

"Mebbe we should think this through," began Raithe, adjusting his coat. "We all been subjected to a deal of stress and strain, and mebbe we should . . . "

"What yuh say, Mister Stryde?" said Sugar. "Yuh got an opinion on this matter? Would yuh mind my company t' Big Bend?"

Stryde sighed as the others turned to face him. "Well, now, yuh sure gotta right t' do as yuh wish, ma'am, and no denyin'. Every man — and woman has. Freedom of choice . . . one of the things we all fight for, ain't it?" His blue eyes sparkled. "As for havin' your company, ma'am . . . I'd say them's just about the warmest words I heard in days!"

Chester Woodley smiled.

Sheriff Brent eased his bulk to one leg.

Doc Maloney coughed lightly.

Isaiah Raithe flicked dust from his coat.

"All aboard for Big Bend," called the conductor.

Reet Morgan threw his unlit cigar to the ground.

And the undertaker hummed.

23

THE night shadows were long and heavy and the warmth of the bar of the Boundless Saloon a soothing balm as Sheriff Brent settled himself in his favourite chair and opened the pages of this week's special edition of the town's newspaper.

THE REMARK BUGLE
Territory of North Dakota
Special Edition
LAST DAYS OF THE DOONES
Town Blazes in Gang Leader's Last Stand
Night Shoot-Out Ends Reign of Terror
Lone Gunman's Vendetta

More than two decades of murder, rape, robbery and pillage were ended in the darkness of a bleak winter's night against the backdrop of a blazing town when Jubal Doone, leader of the notorious Doone gang, was finally gunned down in the snowswept main street . . .

Chester had done a good job, no denying that, thought the sheriff, helping himself to another whiskey. Truthful, thoughtful, no frills, all facts . . . just as it happened, as it was.

Well, it was on record now, there for all to read, and not a hint of prejudice. No favours either; folk were written up as they were and as they reacted, including himself. That was as it should be, just so that generations to come had no misunderstandings. Not that it would put them off building a legend around the events. Oh, sure, they would do that, and no holding them! But history — the real history — would tell it as it unfolded.

Brent grunted. Would bring folk to Remark, no mistake. They would flock here in their droves; hordes of sightseers anxious to walk the very street where Jubal Doone was gunned, stand on the very spot where he fell and died; maybe look for some stain of his blood. Oh, yes, they would do all that; collect the very dirt where the sonofabitch had fallen.

And then, of course, there would be the gun-crazed youngsters who would reckon they could have felled the critter faster — and maybe get to trying to prove it!

He sighed. Busy times ahead. Still, gentlemen of the town committee would be happy enough. Think of the trade, the loose dollars — not to mention the loose women! — and Reet Morgan would embellish the story with the opening of every bottle of his sub-standard hooch!

Pity of it was that Stryde would not be here. Folk would ask about him: who he was, where he came from, where he went to. Brent frowned. "Yeah," he murmured, "where he went."

Never been a word of him since he left town with Sugar. No word out of Big Bend either. Fellow just seemed to have disappeared, the girl with him. Strange . . . well, maybe he was holed-up some place quiet; maybe settling down; farming, homesteading, Sugar alongside of him. She would like that, sure enough. Could be the pair of them might get to marrying and raising a family.

Hell, he was rambling, he thought, shifting in the chair. Did it matter what happened to Stryde? He shifted again. Damn it, of course it did. Without Stryde there would have been no end to the terror of the Doones, and this town no more than a patch of charred dirt. Stryde had done his bit to shape the territory and its future.

History needed men like Stryde.

Still, times moved on. Maybe, once the first flush of the sightseers to Remark had passed, things would get a deal quieter; peaceful, restful, to leave him with the sort of town every sheriff craved, specially when the years were rolling on faster than he cared to remind himself.

All was quiet enough now.

Reet Morgan lounging at the bar, telling his version of the story for the hundredth time. Doc Maloney doing his best to keep Reet to the facts. Isaiah Raithe contemplating in the far corner, wondering just how the town was going to raise the money to rebuild. And the undertaker over there still flicking through his order book. Market in pine coffins had taken something of a slump of late. Long may it be so!

Brent smiled to himself, relaxed in the chair and set himself to wondering if just one more whiskey on this peaceful night might be in order. Could be he should raise a glass to Stryde.

Maybe tomorrow . . .

He sighed, finished his drink and glanced tiredly at the last item on the last page of the *Bugle*'s special edition — and stiffened.

*Drought Threat After Bitter Winter
Water Shortage Fears*

"What the hell!" he croaked, then came to his feet and strode from the bar to the boardwalk with all the menace of a mounting storm.

"Chester Woodley!" he bellowed over the night. "Chester Woodley! This time . . . this time . . . "

THE END

Other titles in the Linford Western Library:

TOP HAND
Wade Everett

The Broken T was big. But no ranch is big enough to let a man hide from himself.

GUN WOLVES OF LOBO BASIN
Lee Floren

The Feud was a blood debt. When Smoke Talbot found the outlaws who gunned down his folks he aimed to nail their hide to the barn door.

SHOTGUN SHARKEY
Marshall Grover

The westbound coach carrying the indomitable Larry and Stretch headed for a shooting showdown.

FIGHTING RAMROD
Charles N. Heckelmann

Most men would have cut their losses, but Frazer counted the bullets in his guns and said he'd soak the range in blood before he'd give up another inch of what was his.

LONE GUN
Eric Allen

Smoke Blackbird had been away too long. The Lequires had seized the Blackbird farm, forcing the Indians and settlers off, and no one seemed willing to fight! He had to fight alone.

THE THIRD RIDER
Barry Cord

Mel Rawlins wasn't going to let anything stand in his way. His father was murdered, his two brothers gone. Now Mel rode for vengeance.

ARIZONA DRIFTERS
W. C. Tuttle

When drifting Dutton and Lonnie Steelman decide to become partners they find that they have a common enemy in the formidable Thurston brothers.

TOMBSTONE
Matt Braun

Wells Fargo paid Luke Starbuck to outgun the silver-thieving stagecoach gang at Tombstone. Before long Luke can see the only thing bearing fruit in this eldorado will be the gallows tree.

HIGH BORDER RIDERS
Lee Floren

Buckshot McKee and Tortilla Joe cut the trail of a border tough who was running Mexican beef into Texas. They stopped the smuggler in his tracks.

BRETT RANDALL, GAMBLER
E. B. Mann

Larry Day had the choice of running away from the law or of assuming a dead man's place. No matter what he decided he was bound to end up dead.

THE GUNSHARP
William R. Cox

The Eggerleys weren't very smart. They trained their sights on Will Carney and Arizona's biggest blood bath began.

THE DEPUTY OF SAN RIANO
Lawrence A. Keating and Al. P. Nelson

When a man fell dead from his horse, Ed Grant was spotted riding away from the scene. The deputy sheriff rode out after him and came up against everything from gunfire to dynamite.